Beverly J James has a passion for people and a passion for writing. She believes that love is the single most important force on the planet. She further believes that love or the *perception* of a lack of love is the driving force behind all actions and reactions of every person on the planet. She assures us that the opposite of love is not hate; rather the opposite of love is apathy. She sends blessings to all living beings. God is love.

For you, Superman. Everything is for and because of you.
You inspire me. You always have. To love.
GOD is Love.

Beverly J James

ALSO KNOWN AS REDEMPTION

AUSTIN MACAULEY PUBLISHERS™
LONDON · CAMBRIDGE · NEW YORK · SHARJAH

Copyright © Beverly J James 2022

The right of Beverly J James to be identified as author of this work has been asserted by the author in accordance with sections 77 and 78 of the Copyright, Designs and Patents Act 1988.

All rights reserved. No part of this publication may be reproduced, stored in a retrieval system, or transmitted in any form or by any means, electronic, mechanical, photocopying, recording, or otherwise, without the prior permission of the publishers.

Any person who commits any unauthorised act in relation to this publication may be liable to criminal prosecution and civil claims for damages.

The story, the experiences, and the words are the author's alone.

A CIP catalogue record for this title is available from the British Library.

ISBN 9781398469600 (Paperback)
ISBN 9781398469624 (ePub e-book)

www.austinmacauley.com

First Published 2022
Austin Macauley Publishers Ltd®
1 Canada Square
Canary Wharf
London
E14 5AA

Special Thanks:

Pierre "Doc 4 Da Streetz" Johnson MD.
Bonnie Linen-Carroll

Chapter 1

(Giselle)

Okay, so my superhero was here. And while I was completely happy for his return, I knew I had to make some adjustments. I did not let him spend the night with me after the party. I wanted to. But here is the thing – I have always felt bad about *my neck*. Seriously.

I have never had a beautiful neck. And I have spent basically a lifetime trying to live with it, without animus. I've never had a beautiful sleek neck that sloped easily into my back and created an illusion of beauty. Instead, it has always had sort of a hump thing that just continued into more back. It really annoyed me and made it hard for me to love that part of me! Wait! Not like the Hunchback of Notre Dame! Not a hunchback, a hunch *neck,* maybe.

It has also created problems for me and a certain sexual position ever since my partner many years ago reached up and put a little squeeze on it during the act! Of all the things he could have done – rubbed my back, held my waist, even slapped my butt! But no! He chose to squeeze the hump in the back of my neck! To be honest I don't know if he was intentionally squeezing it or if in the throes of passion his hand just happened to find it. But I immediately lost whatever ecstasy was involved and just waited for him to finish. I *do* know that I never really got over it. And I never saw him again either. I could never get over the thought of it. Never did doggy style with the light on again – I do not know why, maybe fear that my man would see it and want to touch it. I was undoubtedly traumatised!

Fast forward to now, I still do not like doggy style. Although it has also morphed into a fear of anal. Sorry, not my last hole!!! I just can't do it. But that is another story for another time. I have digressed enough!!!

So back to Kevin…

I needed so much more from him than just showing up in a superman costume.

I had thought of him so many times, imaging us together and completely in love.

When I pushed him out of the door that night the last thing he said was, "Baby, no. I don't want to leave you. I want to stay."

But I kissed him and pushed him out of the door. Then watched him walk down the hallway and leave *me* wanting *him!!!* But I needed it that way.

This morning I was lying in the bed again thinking about him. Knowing that I have these amazing feelings for him, and that he moves my heart and soul, in a way that it had never ever been moved before. So why was I so apprehensive? Why was I… and suddenly he was texting!!!

Him: Good morning, baby.

Me: Good morning (blushing smiley face emoji times three).

Him: (Kiss emoji) You up yet?

Me: I am awake but not up. What about you?

Him: I'm up. Just got out of the shower. Want to get breakfast?

Me: Sure. Meet me at my front door in 20 minutes?

Him: See you then.

I was nervous about him, this superhero of a man. Just the thought of him gave rise to something in my soul that I could not escape. I felt him in my chest, somewhere around my heart, where forever lives. He brought a calmness to me, that everything was alright, that the world itself was a wonderful place.

Again, so why am I so apprehensive? Truth is, I was already so, *so* in love with him, that it was dangerous to me. And apparently, I still did not know that I wanted to be in love. My history of love had already proven that I was not so good at it.

Last night was awesome. We spent amazing time together. We had a few glasses of wine, cuddled on the sofa and watched a movie, well, we talked through the movie. He held my hand at times, stroked the palm with one finger at other times and caressed it at others. We talked almost endlessly about everything.

There was an intimacy and when we came so close to consummating it, I decided to kick him out. Like I said, I needed so much more than him showing up in a superman costume. I was ready to fully give every part of me as never before. I just was not ready to find that it did not take *this* time, as many times before. Clearly that was the reason for the apprehension.

But I was certainly going to keep seeing him! By the way, we did not talk about the ex-wife Michelle yet, I did not want her anywhere in the mix. So, it left me also unsure of where they were now. But in hindsight, I needed to know if crazy had taken her final bow.

(Calvin Baptiste/Gabby)

New Orleans was never kind to Calvin. The Baptiste family was not a winning ticket in life for him. His mother died during his birth and his father never quite recovered from the loss. Calvin often believed that his father hated him because of it, as with Calvin's every misstep, his father reminded him of that fact.

His father had numerous relationships over the years and finally married Carla, when Calvin was eight years old. Unfortunately, his dad's new wife never quite took to him. She and Calvin's mother were once incredibly good friends. But all of that changed drastically. Primarily because they both fell in love with his father and Calvin was the offspring of the apparent winner. He once heard his stepmother complain to his father that Calvin 'made her sick, because he reminded' her of his mother. The foundation of pain and neglect was set without Calvin having done a single thing, other than exist.

There was constant fighting between Carla and his father. And she always said things, awful things to and about Calvin.

His self-esteem grew chronically low, and he learned at an early age not to trust women. Calvin's father died when he was 11 years old. By the time he was 15 he could no longer withstand the abuse lavished upon him for the years preceding, then the years after his father's death. He left.

Calvin was homeless and lived a life in New Orleans struggling, begging and hustling. He lived in shelters, with friends and often on the streets – any place he could safely rest his head. He learned to fight for his life exceedingly early and somehow made it without a home of his own until he was 21 years old. On his 21st birthday something just clicked, he not only wanted more, but he deserved more. New Orleans had never been kind to him. He wanted out. He had saved up enough money to completely leave the state for good. He headed northeast.

While the streets of New Orleans had taught him much more about life itself than any person or book ever could have, the northeast taught him that he could turn *any* woman's head and get her into bed, even though he was not the traditionally handsome guy or pretty boy. But he had that thing, that *Je ne sais quoi*.

He had many relationships, yet he remained faithful to the belief in and was constantly on alert for – his *one*, his soulmate. Because the one thing that life had not stolen from him was his belief in true love and that there was a special person out there just for him. She would love him and allow him to love her. They would have the elusive happily ever after. He still believed.

What he found was relationships that took off then sputtered once a slicker talking, more handsome pretty boy came along. He learned quickly not to invest himself so cursorily, but never gave up at the same time.

Yet, the first time he saw Gabby, he saw what he had been looking for his entire life. He knew it. But he did not know how to make it happen. In the end his antics and attempts to woo and win her heart, left him jobless and in a fight that left him out cold.

He kept having flashbacks of Gabby and that fateful night, even though it had been many weeks since it happened.

This morning his thoughts were of waking up to a swollen left eye and a terrific headache after the altercation with Oliver. He rubbed the left side of his face as though remnants remained. He rose from his bed, sat off the side, dropped his head in his hands and sighed deeply. This was par for the course in his life. He had always worked hard for everything he got. But somehow, he always ended up being punched in the face by life. When his phone rang, he considered not answering it. Then he saw it was the farm calling. He answered.

The male voice on the other end was Travis Sr, (TS).

" Son are you okay?" he asked.

"We really miss you around here. You made a big difference."

Calvin was still mid dismay but was able to fake it.

"Thank you. I'm better and I really miss you all too."

"Calvin, do you think you could come back? Come back and help us out here, son?" TS asked.

Calvin could hear in TS's voice, a strong sense of need and urgency. TS seemed to have no idea about the altercation at The Kitchen. Which was surprising to Calvin. He quit partially because he thought for sure Gabby would have told them. So, he explained that he needed some time to figure out some personal issues in his life.

"We really need you, son."

TS reinforced their need, then patiently waited for a response.

"When do you want me back?" Calvin asked.

"Today or as soon as you can. When *can* you come back, son?" TS eagerly asked.

"I need a couple of days, okay? I need to do some things. I will see you soon though. I will call you when I get back. Okay?" Calvin answered.

"Sure, sure, sure!"

TS quickly agreed and exhaled a deep sigh of relief.

"We will see you as soon as you are ready, son."

Calvin, while rough around the edges and certainly working through issues of his own – had an exceedingly strong work ethic. He also had a huge respect for older people. And he clicked with Travis' parents, TS and his wife Bella from the start. He not only worked for them but frequently assisted with personal errands and even shared advice – from them and to them. He had taken TS to a couple of doctor's appointments and even attended a board meeting with him. They seemed more like the parents he never had than his employers. Yet he never knew of the full relationship they had with Gabby. He had never shared the feelings he had for Gabby or the true depth of troubles of his own life.

Calvin hung up the phone and made a mental note.

"Things I need to do before going back – shave, get a haircut, a smile and a way to explain my actions to Gabby before I can peacefully return. I must somehow *redeem* myself."

Chapter 2

(Gabby's Awakening)

Lola could hardly wait for her mum to turn off the car, to open the door and jump out. She could see her dad through the windows of The Kitchen and made a quick and straight shot for him. She opened the double doors to the building, her long red hair bouncing as she ran and jumped in his arms.

"Daddy! Daddy!" she shouted.

Oliver picked his four-year-old daughter up and swung her around, giving her a little kiss.

"Hi, sweetheart! Daddy did not know you were coming. Where's Mummy?" he asked still holding her, who was perhaps one of the prettiest little girls Gabby, (who was standing at the register near Oliver) had seen in quite some time.

Oliver looked at Gabby as the doors opened again and Lynne walked in and kissed him.

"She wanted to see you," Lynne explained.

Gabby was not at all interested in this clearly happy family reunion. But just as she turned to go to her office, Oliver called her over.

"Gabby, wait. You got a minute?" Oliver asked.

Dammit! she thought. *This cannot be good for me.* She stopped in her tracks, took a brief pause then turned to re-join them.

"Gabby, meet my daughter, Lola, and my *wife*, Lynne," Oliver said with lingering eye contact, which Gabby broke.

Gabby playfully said hello to Lola commenting on how pretty she was. Then shaking Lynne's hand.

"Nice to finally *officially* meet you, Lynne."

"You too, Gabby. And thanks for hiring Oliver. It's been tough for a few months," Lynne added.

"But we've made it, right, Oli?" she said looking at Oliver.

"Do you mind if I take a few minutes?" Oliver asked Gabby.

"No, no, not at all. Take your time," Gabby said starting back to her office.

"Daddy, can I see where you cook?" Lola excitedly asked.

"Sure, baby!"

He never put her down. The family headed to the back.

Gabby had elected not to investigate the true scoop with Oliver and Lynne. She could tell herself anything if she did not know the truth. But now, this truth… this… this inescapable avalanche of truth had punched her in her head. She was dizzy, off balance.

She did not know what to think, do or feel. She was no longer free to pretend; she knew that the conversation was now inevitable. And she also knew she was not ready for it. She honestly did not want to care about it. But she did care. A lot. An awful lot in fact.

This knowledge proved that all the time he had given her, was nothing but lies. All the emotions he had consistently shown her, more lies. Everything she felt, though perhaps the absolute best feelings she'd had in an exceedingly long time

– were all based on lies. Every touch, every intimacy, everything, nothing but lies. Oliver was an apparently happily married man (well, at least his wife seemed to think so anyway) with a family that clearly loved him.

Gabby walked to the window and stared out, shaking her head.

"Wow, just wow!"

She took a very deep breath then slowly went to her office. She closed the door while leaning her forehead on it then began to sob quietly.

Suddenly there were three very loud knocks on her door. Startled, she opened the door without wiping her face.

Oliver stepped in and with one single move pulled her into his arms and kissed her until she found herself kissing him more passionately than ever.

"Please, Oliver..." she said, "please don't stop, don't stop loving me! Please!"

In midst of kissing her, he paused, looked into her eyes, and said, "I can never stop, baby, I can never stop loving you! It is not a possibility, baby. Not possible."

The time was now, he reached behind them and locked the door. He continued kissing her while carrying her to the desk. She felt him reach under her flowing white dress and remove her underwear. They never stopped kissing. When he entered her body, she had a huge sigh of relief, the stress dissipated.

(Greta's Quad Screening)

Greta and Cameron were on their way to her obstetrician Dr Kenya Embers. Today they would, if they desired, find out the sex of the baby. But more importantly there was news on the results of her Quad Screening, though she initially did not expect bad news, the fact that they had to come in to receive the results had her deeply concerned.

Greta loved the way Cam always held her hand as he drove. She got in and fastened her seatbelt. He was there, car running. No movement.

"Are you forgetting something?" he asked.

"What?"

She feigned.

He vigorously waved his empty hand for her to take and hold.

She laughed.

"Like we couldn't leave without you holding my hand!"

She laughed.

"We *could.*"

He quickly admitted.

"I just do not *want* to."

They laughed.

He leant over, kissed her and gently caressed her tummy, their baby.

When they arrived at the doctors' office, Cameron opened her car door and helped her out as usual – but stopped briefly before they went in.

"Do you want to know what we are having?" he asked.

"In a way I don't," she said. "But in a way I do. I really want to prepare. It has been so hard not to do things. I have been so ready to shop and plan for weeks! Now that I can find out, I don't know if I can wait any longer!" She admitted. "What about you, Cam, do you want to wait?"

He kissed her. He looked her eyes and shook his head in perhaps a surreal disbelief.

"So many times, I hear people say all I want is a healthy child. And it never resonated with me before," he said. "And it's true, I want a healthy child as much as the next guy. But, babe, I think I want to know now what we are having too."

Greta dropped her head. Cam could see her starting to lose it and embraced her.

"It's okay, baby. Everything is okay," he said. "Do you understand?"

He raised her head with his hand beneath her chin and repeated the question, "Do you understand?"

Greta shrugged her shoulders a bit then uttered a reluctant "Yes" followed by a more realistic "But what if it's not?"

"Then we will handle it together."

He kissed her forehead.

"I love you, Cam" (she paused and gave thought to this amazing man). "Baby, thank you."

Cameron quickly added, "No, baby, thank you! Thank you for being my wife. Thank you for making me a father. And, baby, most of all, thank you for loving me. I promise you, babe, together we can handle everything, not just anything, but everything."

"I love you, Cam," she said. "I love you so much."

They embraced in love and hope.

They had the first appointment of the day and were taken directly to Dr Embers's office after completing the registration. When they walked in the office, she was there waiting for them.

"Good morning. Have a seat."

Dr Embers pointed to the two chairs across from her huge, file covered ornate mahogany desk.

"I'm not going to play with you guys or sugar-coat this. The tests came back positive for the Trisomy 21 abnormality. Your baby has Down's Syndrome."

Neither of them said a word or took their eyes off her. Cameron had taken Greta's hand as they sat – and he held it, just a bit tighter.

Dr Embers continued, "At this point we need to do a more detailed ultrasound and look for additional abnormalities. The other thing I want to do is set you up with a MFM or a Maternal Foetal Medicine specialist. I know someone, she is one of the top specialists in the field."

"How quickly can you do that?" Greta asked as tears slowly crept from her eyes.

"Likely within this week or early next week. I will get her to work you in." she said and passed a box of tissues to Cameron, who in turn removed a couple and passed them to Greta.

She began to sob audibly. She placed her head in her hands, leant into her own lap, inconsolable.

"It's okay, baby."

Cam attempted to console her, though the initial shock had him nearly inconsolable as well.

Greta looked up at Dr Embers.

"What else could be wrong? What else are we looking for?" Greta asked.

"Again, I'm not going to sugar-coat this. I am going to be completely honest with you. But I don't want you to get so worried about things before we really know."

"I understand." Greta said. She then looked at Cameron and added, "*We* understand." Nodding her head.

"Okay," said Dr Embers, "we are going to do a detailed Ultrasound. We are going to focus on everything, the brain, the heart, the lungs, all of the organs. We will do a thorough exam. We may find nothing, and it is not unusual to find nothing. But we are going to be sure. We are going to look for everything. Okay?"

"Okay," they answered in unison.

"Come with me", Dr. Embers said and led them to the exam room.

Cameron sat near her holding her hand during the entire exam. He had never missed an appointment and he never would. Now was the moment they had been waiting for. Her doctor began to squeeze the lubricant on her abdomen, then began to move the probe around the lower portion of it.

"You see that flicker there?" the doc asked.

"Yes," they both answered together.

"That's your baby's heartbeat," she said, then asked, "Do you want to know the sex?"

Cam and Greta looked at each other and said in an appearingly pre-planned manner, "Yes!"

Dr Embers, absorbed and relished the information, then looked at the two of them.

"You have a son."

Chapter 3

(Calvin/Gabby)

Calvin knew he would not get an answer by calling Gabby on her cell or at work. He knew if he was to talk to her, he had to revert to old faithful. Waiting for her to appear, while headed to work. He sat in his car early in the morning and waited for her to arrive. Of course, Oliver arrived first.

Calvin sat there for an additional hour before Gabby made it there. When he first saw her, his initial thoughts were to forget about it. He felt a rushing in his chest and a real fear of complete rejection torturing his mind.

"Sometimes," he said out loud, "you have to do what you have to do. Even through the fear. Come what may."

Calvin got out of his car and begin to approach Gabby. When Gabby saw him, she did not flinch.

"I knew you would show up sooner or later," she said.

"Okay. I'm here," he said.

"Do you see this?"

She removed a can of pepper spray from her purse, hand positioned to fire.

"I swear to God, first I'm going pepper spray you until I blind your ass. Then I am going to tase you until you flatline! Do you understand?" she vehemently asked.

Calvin stopped moving.

"I deserve that. I deserve your anger. I deserve your mistrust. But are you willing to give me three minutes?"

"Three minutes for what?"

She almost shouted. "For what Calvin? "To tell me what this time, maybe I have AIDS as well as Herpes? Or is there something even worse you want to tell me or do to me? Three minutes for what?"

Calvin took a deep breath, adjusted his thoughts to ensure he was quiet and non-threatening and said, "To explain. To ask for forgiveness."

"Well. Just stay exactly where you are and say whatever you need to say, Calvin!" She kept her pepper spray visible.

He took another deep breath and readjusted himself.

"I was so wrong," he said, "and I'm sorry."

She did not respond.

"I'm sure it doesn't seem like it, but you are actually pretty important to me." He said and shook his head. "I'm sorry. I won't go through all of it, but do you remember all the endless conversations we used to have?"

"You mean the conversations before you told me I had Herpes and started a fight with my chef, inside my place of business! Yeah, Calvin, I do! What about them?"

"That's fair. I deserve that too," he said. "You have a right to still be angry. But then, before all the bad stuff – did you see something in me, something in *me and you* that mattered before I ruined it?"

Gabby did not respond, but on the inside, she felt it. She did. She had only allowed one other man to touch her in her entire lifetime, before Calvin. *Of course,* he had mattered to her. But that was before. She held her chin high and refused to answer.

"You don't have to answer that," Calvin said. "I am sorry I shouldn't have even asked. Thing is, TS asked me to come back, and I will be back at the farm starting tomorrow. I wanted to be the first to tell you. I did not want you to be surprised to see me. And if I need to avoid coming here, I need to know that too. Whatever you say, I'll do."

"I already knew you were coming back, Calvin! Why do you think I have pepper spray? Bella told me, even before they asked you!" She not so politely informed him.

"And you didn't tell them not to have me back?"

"No," she said, shaking her head a bit. "They believe in you. And they don't know about us. So, don't tell them! And as far as your coming here, fine. But do not give me a reason to stop you! Because I will stop you, in a heartbeat. Do you understand?"

"I'm sorry for everything. You never deserved any of that. It was all me. All my fault. But maybe things are not always as they seem. Honestly, I just thought I needed to know why you shut me out of your life. I'm really sorry."

With that, he turned and headed back to his car.

"Gabby!" he yelled turning around as he arrived at his car. "Have a great day!"

Gabby decided not to care. She was over it. She did not look back or respond. She just kept walking to The Kitchen.

(Greta/Cameron)

The ride back home from the doctor's office was quiet. No reassurances that everything was going to be alright from either of them. No questions on how the other felt. No overt tears or emotions. But he held her hand and every now and then, he would squeeze it, just a little bit.

When they arrived, he parked in the driveway – Cameron leant his head on the steering wheel. Greta extended her hand and placed it on the back of his head. She began rubbing down to the base of his neck. She moved closer to him and pressed her forehead on his right temple.

"I'm so sorry, baby," she whispered.

She noticed tears streaming down his face and lifted it towards her and began to kiss them away.

"I know what this means to you, Cam. But I refuse to believe this is going to be a sad story for us. We have to believe, okay."

He looked up to her, in her eyes. Then dropped his head again.

"Baby, we can handle this." Greta assured him. "Okay?"

She began to cry.

"But I cannot do it without you, Cam. I just cannot. I am going to need you to be okay with whatever we face, baby. Okay?"

"Okay," he said, looking at her again. "I understand. I promise you I am not going anywhere. I swear I will always be here for our family, no matter what happens. I just need a minute to grasp it."

"I know Cam, I know," she said.

They held each other, fully embraced, seated in the front seat of the car – crying… for a few more minutes.

(Giselle)

I was constantly thinking about the fact that I had not had sex with Kevin yet. We were never intimate before the breakup, we had been back together since Halloween and it would be Thanksgiving in a few days, and nada. We had come close to it, but I just had not been able to do it yet. I was not trying to do a 90 day or whatever challenge. It was just *something*. And it's more than just the neck thing. I have not had sex in YEARS!!! Honestly, in more than a decade and a half. So much so that my body started to take care of itself, and I would wake up in the middle of the night mid orgasm! I could not possibly tell him that. I was just not ready yet. I called a meeting with the girls, and waited for them to arrive – late!

Greta arrived first. When I opened the door, her eyes were red and swollen. The typically put together Greta, was only a sympathetic 'Hey, what's wrong?' away from falling into my arms in tears.

My initial thought was that something had happened to Cameron. I held her tight and allowed her that moment. She broke the embrace, wiped her tears with her bare hands, walked further in and sobbed.

"Something is wrong with the baby, G" she said.

I closed to door and walked over to the sofa where she had sat herself on the floor and rested her head on the cushion.

I did not know what *this* was, but it was certainly far more than my fear of having sex with my superhero! Okay, I could wait.

I sat on the floor next to her.

"What's wrong with the baby?"

She looked up to me, shook her head and cried even more.

"Greta! Talk to me!" I somewhat demanded.

She looked at me and made a fake laugh.

"Thanksgiving. Thanksgiving," she said.

She was clearly in deep thought.

Just then the doorbell rang. I could not remember if I locked the door or not. I went and opened it without looking at Gabby, grabbed a box of tissues and returned to Greta.

Gabby instinctively sat on the floor with us.

"What's wrong, guys?" she inquired.

I looked at her, shrugging my shoulders and shaking my head.

Greta wiped her eyes with the tissue, and visibly attempted to collect herself.

"Well," she placed her hands on her baby bump and began to caress it. "The baby has Down's Syndrome. Please do not tell me about children with Down's Syndrome. I already know. And I am not afraid to raise this baby. But there could be more. We don't know yet."

"Greta," I whispered empathetically.

I wanted to say something comforting and profound. No chance. I do not think Bridget would have been able to say something here that helped.

Gabby reached in and gave her a hug and soon we were in our trademark three-way embrace.

Between heaving and tears Greta said, "There is a possibility of more abnormalities in the foetus. We do not know yet. We must do more testing."

"I'm so sorry, Greta," Gabby said. "I wish there were something I could do."

"There's nothing anyone can do right now. Just what we are doing." Greta still crying said in full despair. "Nothing at all…"

Despair filled the entire room. Quiet, unfiltered despair.

I didn't know what to do so I blurted out, "I have not had sex in more than 15 years!"

They both pulled back and looked me as though I had suddenly grown a second head!

"Damn." Gabby said initially somewhat quietly.

Then she crafted a loud, full of disbelief, leaning way back and looking at me.

"DAMN!"

"Really, Gabby! It's not *that* much of breaking news!" I said somewhat offended.

"Oh, it's breaking news alright" she sputtered.

We all stopped hugging. I looked at Greta, stood up and helped her up from the floor.

"I'm sorry," I said looking at Greta. "I just didn't know what else to say."

"It's okay," she said blowing her nose. "I didn't either. Cam and I didn't even speak on the way home."

Gabby was holding Greta's hand, snot and all.

"So, what's the next step?" Gabby asked.

"We are going to see a specialist. We haven't gotten the appointment date yet. They are going to check for everything, every system, be sure that there are no other abnormalities."

She started to cry again.

"You know the worst part of all of this? I am afraid of how it could affect Cam. I feel like I need to keep him okay in all of this. What if he starts to drink again?"

"Come on, Greta, that is so ridiculous!" Gabby blurted out, perhaps without thought. "Why? Give him some credit. Believe in him. Trust him."

"He's a different kind of man. I don't know, I'm worried." Greta admitted.

"Cam loves you!" I said, somewhat in disbelief that she even had concerns about him. Everything that I knew about Cam, he would handle it.

"I'm not saying that he doesn't love me. I know that he does. But there are things that you don't know about him. But I do. I know what he needs. I know what scares him. I know what makes him lose himself. I cannot let that happen." She said with complete candour through tears and distress. "I have to take care of him too."

"The fact that you know all of that," I said, "is what will help him through and you as well. I know he is worried about you too."

I thought to myself how amazing she was to consider *him* at this time. I could not even get over my neck! So, I wanted to forget the conversation about me and the sexless last more than 15 years of my life. But NO!!!

Gabby did a full body turn toward me and as though it was impossible to fathom again and said, "Please explain to me, not *why*, but HOW is it that you have not had sex in more than 15 years, G!!! Really? And what have you been doing with Kevin?"

Gabby quickly answered herself.

"Never mind, I know – nothing!!!"

She laughed. Then nodded at me to answer.

"I think," I said, "I got so involved in work and after being hurt the last time, I just did not want it anymore. Pretty soon it became way of life."

I pondered. "I didn't even miss it" I said.

"I don't get it." She added, "You are around all those doctors, surgeons, male nurses! Nothing made you just a little hot in more than 15, *FIFTEEN YEARS?*"

"I did not say that. I said I have not had sex in more than 15 years. I did not say that I had not wanted to! That's two different things," I said correcting her.

Greta found a way to chime in, even amidst her despair.

"So, what have you and Kevin been doing? I know it's 2022, but is he okay with a sexless relationship? Or are you giving the man something – a hand, a tongue, something?"

Before I could answer Gabby jumped in.

"I know what you are doing."

She smirked and nodded her head.

"You are giving him some tongue action! Right?"

"No, I'm not! But if I wanted to, I would. I'm just not ready," I explained.

"WHY???" they both asked in perfect unison.

"I thought you were in love with him," Gabby said then quickly added, "by the way, it's okay that you are not having sex. It's not something to be ashamed of or anything. It's your body. Your body, your choice. You know, do as you please. But since you brought it up! Are you waiting for something special to happen?"

"Well, I'm hesitant for more reasons than one" I answered. "But I do not know that my body will fit it… you know… nothing has been in there for so long. What if it is like a virgin again? What if it will not go in?"

"Is that a thing? Can that happen?" Greta asked.

"Yes! It's absolutely a thing!" I said, then giving a bit more thought. "I think it's a thing."

"Then buy a dildo!" Gabby blurted out. "A big one! That will tell you! And you will not have to be afraid. You will find out by yourself!"

We all thought for a few seconds.

That was not a bad idea.

"I don't know how to shop for a dildo or even the first place to look!" I said.

Smacking her lips Gabby proudly said, "I do!"

We started to laugh.

"Okay," I said.

And I thought to myself, *This could work for that problem. But what about my neck?*

Now let us be honest here – almost everybody has a neck issue when it comes to our bodies. Whether it's actually your neck or your nose being too sharp or blunt, or your eyes are too wide, or you have big feet, a flat butt or a big fat stomach or skinny legs – not what other people think of us – just our own thoughts. Mine, my thoughts are of my neck, (even now).

But while I was ruminating about my neck, I looked at my friend Greta and noticed that she had started to cry again. My neck thoughts went out the window.

I leant my head against hers.

"It's going to be alright," I said.

She nodded and said, "It *has* to be. That is what I need in my life right now. I need it to be alright. No more health issues, for my son. It's a boy."

"Wow. That's really great… right?" I said looking to Gabby to chime in.

"It really is. We got you, Greta. And everything *is* going to be alright. Trust!" Gabby said, as we all again entered the 3G, three-way hug.

"We just have to keep the faith, hope, belief and find a dildo for Giselle!" Greta added with an unconvincing laugh.

Chapter 4

(Oliver/Gabby)

The relationship between Gabby and Oliver had gone from amazing, to pained with deep regret and disbelief. She knew there was another woman in his life, but he gave her what she needed and somehow that seemed to be all that mattered. Now she could barely stand the sight of him and only spoke to him when it was necessary.

They were getting a shipment from the farm today. Calvin would be coming. She needed to tell Oliver, but she didn't want to talk to him. She sat at her desk trying to figure out a way not to talk to him.

An email. A note on the prep table. Suddenly a loud knock on the door.

Gabby was startled and quickly said, "Come in!"

Oliver slowly stuck his head in the door first, then slowly entered.

"Can we talk?"

"Of course. Sit," she said as though disaffected.

"I want to talk about us," he said.

"Apparently, Oliver, there is no *us*. Look, no biggie," she said, still disaffected.

She began to work on her computer – at least feign working on her computer.

"She gave up everything for me," he said.

Gabby did not look up.

"The fact that I'm married does not change how I feel about you, about us. But you need to understand that she sacrificed everything she had for me," he said.

Gabby looked at him and asked, "And I need to know this, *why*?"

"Because I'm never going to leave her," he said. "I am never going to leave my family. Do you understand?"

Pause in the room – Gabby had no air.

He reiterated "Do you understand?"

"Do *you* understand that I'm not asking you to leave your family? I'm asking you to prep for Thanksgiving dinner. Or are you no longer willing to do that either?" (She was highly annoyed at his audacity!)

"I was a runaway, criminal background. I learned to cook in prison. I met her when I got out. She was younger than me, still living with her parents but 19 years old. I…"

Gabby cut him off by saying, "I really don't care, Oliver! How can I make you understand that?"

"Just listen! I need you to know this!!!" He had raised his voice, annoyed and insistent.

"What if I don't want to know?" she shot back.

"Are you trying to ease your own mind or mine?"

"I'm trying to tell you that I love you." He said. "But I am also trying to tell you why I can never leave Lynne. Please let me. If I ever mattered to you. Just let me explain. Please…"

"Just hurry okay. And I need to tell you something too…"

"You are making this really hard for me," he said.

Gabby did not respond but looked directly at him.

He continued.

"I met her at a time when I was really lost. When I didn't matter on any level to anybody. It was funny because when I met her, she had everything. The only child of extremely well to do parents. She had a better car when she was sixteen than I did when we met and even now. But she saw something in me that no one had ever seen before. She saw something good in me and helped me to see good in myself. She wanted me to meet her parents. Being six years older than her wasn't bad enough for her parents so they did a background check. They demanded that we break up. I knew that I was not good enough for her. I knew they were right. But she refused to stop seeing me, even when I tried. She left home and moved in with me. But her parents called the police and said I was holding her hostage. I was arrested. But I was not on paper. I had served all my time and was flat. Lynne made sure law enforcement knew I was not holding her hostage and that she was there of her own free will. But things only got worse with her parents. Her father threatened me physically. In the end we decided to leave town. She had money in the bank she took it all. She was forced by her parents to return her car to them. She only had very few clothes. But she and I had each other. We have been through being completely broke, pregnancy, a new-born, living in and out of shelters, multiple jobs and losing them. Just everything. But she never left me. She never gave up on me. She could have. But she always stood by me."

"And you pay her back by having an affair with me?"

"I fell in love with you the first moment I saw you."

"You knew you were married, and you knew we could never be together. Yet you pursued me. Why?"

Gabby was angry and let it show in her voice.

"I was supposed to. I was supposed to be there for you, and I was supposed to love you. I still love you," he said.

"Do you love your wife?"

She did not ask as a normal course of questioning. She really wanted to know.

"Yes. I do," he said in full candour. "But not like I love you."

"Well, *that* is for damn sure! You don't want to be with me!"

Shaking his head Oliver leant in toward the desk.

"And, Gabby, you know that's not true. I want you more than everything. But I am not the man who can just abandon his family for anything – even for the most pure and true love I have ever known, Gabby. I can't do it."

The room was quiet.

"Do you understand what she has sacrificed for me? For us?" he asked attempting to put the situation in perspective.

Gabby chose not to answer, rather give him information she knew he needed before it became a surprise and possibly a problem.

"Calvin is back at the farm. He'll be coming soon with some Thanksgiving supplies," she said with nearly a sting and conscious intent to wound.

"WHAT?"

Oliver was shocked.

"Are you kidding me?

"Nope."

"How long have you known that he was back? Are you seeing him again? Did he call you? How do you know?"

Oliver could not release his rapid-fire questions fast enough nor wait for an answer.

"Bella told me that they needed him. Apparently, he was amazing to them. They didn't want to let him go. You understand that. Right? Someone too amazing to let go?"

She again attempted an insignificant but significant wound.

"Really? Okay. I see. Have you talked to him?" he asked.

"Yes."

Gabby looked back at the computer feigning work again.

Oliver sinks back into the chair, shakes his head.

"When?"

"Been a day or so" she said nonchalantly.

"And you are just now telling me? What if he had come by?"

"He did."

She did not look up.

"Gabby! Look at me! What happened?"

Oliver could feel himself growing furious.

"Nothing. We talked. We came to an understanding."

She briefly glanced at him, then back to the computer.

"How could you *not* tell me this? What the fu…" Gabby interrupted.

"Well, you made it kind of hard for me to do that with the whole family thing Oliver!"

Oliver stood.

"I gotta go."

He left the office.

Gabby watched him get up and walk away, closing the door, just short of a slam.

She thought to herself, *What a fool I am.* She felt the emotion rise in her chest and the tears attempted to start again.

She said, "NOPE! No tears!"
And she stopped.

(Greta/Cameron)

The MFM – Maternal Foetal Medicine specialist, while quite accomplished and highly recommended caught them a bit off guard when she walked into the exam room. She did not look older than twenty-one or twenty-two, certainly not twenty-five. Her white lab coat and forest green scrubs gave her some credibility, but somehow this small African American female, was not at all what they were expecting.

She approached Cameron first shaking his hand.

"I'm Dr K'Sennia Jordan."

Then to Greta.

"Good morning, how are you?"

"I'm okay, we are okay (caressing her tummy). You?" Greta answered.

"I'm great, thanks for asking."

Dr Jordan sat and began to look at the chart she had brought with her.

"So today, we are going to do a significantly detailed Ultrasound. We are looking for anything and everything. We may find nothing; we may find something. Are you ready?"

She stood and removed her lab coat revealing what appeared to be a pregnant belly.

"Wow," Greta said. "May I ask you a personal question Dr Jordan?"

She had picked up the ultrasound probe, stopped and held it to answer Greta.

"Yes, sure."

"Are you pregnant?"

Dr Jordan laughed. "Yes, I am." She laughed again. "I thought you were going to ask me my age!"

She exposed Greta's belly.

"Well, now that you mention it," Greta said.

"Well, I am 27 years old. Everything about my education was accelerated, from my graduating high school at 16, college just before my 19th birthday and on and on. Most people want to know my age before my credentials."

She added the gel that she intentionally instructed her staff to keep warm.

"Did you find out the sex of your child yet?" The doctor asked.

"Yes. We had initially decided to wait, but things changed a bit, rather quickly," Greta said.

Dr. Jordan shared "My husband and I have a reveal party planned." Then she hesitated, looking intently at the ultrasound screen.

"Just a moment," she said.

She began taking pictures and expanding certain areas on the screen then taking pictures of those as well.

Both Greta and Cameron found themselves completely quiet as Dr Jordan was completely focused, offering no play by play. The entire exam took just over an hour. Dr Jordan wiped Greta's tummy and said,

"I want to see you both Monday morning at 8 a.m. I will tell the front desk. You don't need to do anything else, just get dressed and I will see you then."

She began to wash her hands.

"Is there something wrong?" Cameron asked.

"I want to completely go through everything. I do not want to give you something to worry about needlessly. Nor give you false hope. I will tell you everything I know after I thoroughly examine everything, okay?"

They both nod in agreement but look at each other for comfort. Something was not right. Tomorrow was Thanksgiving. So, they would see her first thing Monday morning. Neither of them knew what to expect.

Dr Jordan smiled a bit.

"Enjoy your Thanksgiving holiday."

She then left the room.

(Calvin/Gabby/Oliver)

Early morning the day before Thanksgiving, Calvin returned to The Kitchen for the first time since the fiasco with Oliver. He considered as he was driving the supply truck, how he would react. In his soul, he wanted to beat Oliver to a pulp. And even though he had been knocked out with one punch, he was not at all discouraged or without belief in himself. That being said – Oliver had to not be a factor in his life in anyway. He only represented a distraction that could be very costly.

Calvin considered apologising. But decided – not to. Just do what he had to do and get out.

Calvin backed the truck up to the receiving dock, hopped out and banged on the door to alert them of his arrival.

Oliver knew sooner or later he would meet face to face with Calvin again. He did not like the thought of it, not to mention the reality of it. As he walked to the back door, he felt his heart begin to race. He took a deep breath unlatched and opened the back door.

Oliver had fully made himself ready to see Calvin's face, but instead Rick, the assistant was there to block the door and start the unload. Today's delivery was smaller than usual, just to do a little extra for the community. Calvin decided to return to the truck and allow Rick and Oliver to unload. Rick had Oliver sign, before they left.

Calvin was not ready. He was not afraid. He just was not ready. Besides, they had to return on Monday with full food supplies.

Chapter 5

(Giselle)

I was completely stuck in my own head about my neck. But I also knew how much Kevin wanted some deeper form of intimacy. He didn't push me and certainly didn't demand it, but he made me know how much he wanted us closer. I wondered if by not finding a way to give him some form of relief, if maybe I would begin to push him away. I couldn't tell him about my neck right now and I had not checked myself out with a dildo. So, I thought maybe I could, perhaps I could ease a bit of fellatio in. Every man loves that right?

At any rate, I had decided that I really wanted to make Kevin feel good. He had been so patient with me, even when he was so hard that he could have used his penis for a jack hammer. So, I was going to give him a little head. It was his first night back from the station and I knew how difficult this had been for him. I wasn't sure exactly when, but that is what I was going to do.

So, I had been sitting there practicing with a banana. I know it is a cliché, and I have done it before, fellatio that is – I guess it should be just like riding a bike. Seemed like I was doing it right. In. Out. Lick it a little. Kiss it. Focus on the head. I could do it. Oh damn! Doorbell! He was here.

(Softening Hearts)

Calvin/Gabby

When her phone rang, the last name Gabby expected to see was 'Super Asshole' the name on Calvin's number in her phone, and she had for some reason forgotten that she'd unblocked him. Calvin was equally not expecting to get through and most certainly not expecting her to answer.

She answered in a manner that would likely have made a lesser man hang up the phone without a word. "What? Calvin!!!"

Calvin laughed into the phone and said, "So you unblocked me?"

"Seems simple enough you may need to contact me regarding your job, with strong emphasis on YOUR JOB! What do you want, Calvin?" she asked with full intent to demonstrate that she had no time for anything other than business.

"I'm coming in tomorrow. You know Bella wanted some more things delivered on Thanksgiving Day, right?"

"Of course, I know that," she quickly said.

"And I'm coming by myself. I am coming inside. Let your boy know. Because I don't want any trouble out of him. Or anybody for that matter," he said.

"I've already told him that you're back and he is fine with it. Just do your job. Anything else?" she asked with a bit of a snap.

"Nope."

Then he quickly added, "As a matter of fact, yes!"

"Spit it out, Calvin!"

She had little patience for him, but knew she needed to work with him and at least try to be cordial.

Calvin took a deep breath and quietly made a request.

"Forgive me."

"See you tomorrow, Calvin."

She hung up.

She regretted that there was something about him that did something to her, even with all they had been through. She wondered if it had something to do with this madness with Oliver and his married ass. She was not sure. But she was sure that it was something.

(Tapping Out)

There were many things that I really liked about Kevin, but I was so enamoured with his kitchen skills. He loved cooking and cleaning simultaneously. The man could finish a multi course meal, clean every dish used to prepare the meal and have everything packed for refrigeration as leftovers, before the food even remotely cooled! And there was simply something magical in watching this amazing firefighter chop vegetables and look heroic. Wow. He had this cucumber, apple, lemon juice with a little touch of salt, that tonight he added watermelon to – that was simply delicious. Truth is, I never would have thought of that combination, and I really do not know if it was delicious or if he was… I just knew that I wanted to make him feel like a king, I wanted to serve him, please him, relieve him. I really did.

This was my chance.

As we lay together on this huge sofa with my head on his chest, I looked up to him and turned his face toward mine and kissed him. I kissed him with passion and intent. I started with a gentle kiss to his chin, went down his neck. I kissed him on every part of his neck slowly and deliberately.

"Baby," I said looking up at him, "take off your shirt, okay?"

He looked at me for a couple of beats as though to register in his brain what was about to happen. Then in the quickest of moments, he removed his pullover and quickly returned to his initial resting position.

I was not sure who enjoyed it more, him or me but as I kissed his entire chest and moved my hand down to open his pants, I could feel his heart racing. I kissed him farther down to his navel and I felt his body moving in anticipation. I touched him. He was so hard, so big. I felt myself starting to want him inside of me. But I needed to taste him.

I put my hand inside of his underwear just enough to bring the head only out. I breathed on it very warmly. I touched the smoothness of such incredible hardness as his body began to writhe in deeper anticipation.

This was a chance I was willing to take. After all we had both been tested for STDs, not only came back completely clean but also promised celibacy to each other.

I took a taste, a small taste. A slow, wet, warm taste. He relaxed as to give me full access. I accepted. I felt myself taking him into my mouth and caressing him with my tongue in such a way that he was enjoying it, and it was worth the wait.

I had expected him to cum quickly because he had been waiting for so long, but he did not. I knew I needed to do more and make him feel it and he would grab the back of my head of almost choke me with that giant thing. But he did not. He did move in a way that I thought he was enjoying it every now and then, but overall, I did not get the response I expected. But I did not give up.

I tried the deep throat thing, taking in as much as I could at one time. Maybe not a good idea. He pulled away a bit.

I was not going to give up, I began to move faster and try to pleasure him more and more.

Finally, he tapped me on my shoulder and said, "Baby, I do not think it is going to happen."

I was hurt.

"Baby, what is wrong?" I asked, feeling completely rejected.

"Nothing. I just do not think I am going to cum right now. I love you for trying, babe."

"Please babe, let me…" I asked, unsure as to why he stopped me.

"No. I just don't want to right now. I just don't want to. You don't *have* to do this, is all," he explained.

I stopped and sort of wiped my mouth. I wished I could have disappeared.

He could tell how disappointed I was. And pulled me back up to his chest and just held me.

What a disaster!!!

Even here in his arms I still wish I could crawl away or disappear.

We went to bed and when I woke, he was in the shower. I heard odd noises, as though he was in pain when the water stopped.

"Are you okay, babe?" I asked, going into the bathroom.

I walked in to find him looking at and somewhat nursing his penis as he dried it.

He looked up at me without saying a word.

"Baby. You good?"

He shook his head indicating no.

"Baby you cut me up with your teeth last night. I'm bit up as hell!"

My eyes exploded to the size of lemons.

"Yikes! Why didn't you tell me?"

"Well, I did," he said.

"I mean why didn't you stop me before THIS!" I asked pointing to his obviously damaged penis.

I didn't understand.

"Because I know you were doing it for me, baby. I know you were doing it because you love me."

"I do love you, Kevin, but I don't want to hurt you."

I shook my head at myself.

"Dammit!"

He walked over and kissed me. Then held me with a gentle sway.

"I love you," he said, "and I know you are definitely not out there do this all of the time!"

He then snickered very softly into my ear and bit the lobe just a little bit.

Glad he found it sort of funny.

But I believed him. He could see beyond my inept attempt at fellatio. And I loved him more at that moment than I have ever loved any person in my entire life.

I attempted to touch that thing a little bit, but he quickly jumped back and said, "Nope! Stay away until I tell you it is okay to touch it!"

Okay. I can do that. Besides, today is Thanksgiving and we are going to cook together. I am a bit excited to see how that is going to go.

(Gabby and Calvin)

On the other side of town, Calvin was pulling up to the back door of The Kitchen to make an additional delivery for the Thanksgiving meal. Thanksgiving over the years had greatly increased in numbers and with the pandemic and economy, Bella and TS wanted to have great certainty that the need for the community was met and decided to send a second truck.

Calvin raised his head and looked around pensively before getting out of the truck. He was alone. This delivery was all his. He was ready to face, well, whatever. He had backed the truck to the delivery dock and refused to delay the inevitable. He jumped out and banged on the back door, then stepped away and raised the rear hatch of the truck.

Oliver opened the door. Just seeing Calvin caused his anxiety to rise. He propped the door open and initially stepped away from the back door to return to the prep area.

But Oliver stopped himself. He shook his head as he thought of what is more important.

Walking back to the door he asked, "You need any help, man?"

"No. I got it."

Calvin answered never looking up.

Calvin brought four large boxes. As he placed the last box on the floor Gabby walked in.

When their eyes met, something happened. They both knew it and instinctively broke the trance and looked away. But not before holding the eye contact for more than a couple of seconds.

"We will put it away. Thank you," Gabby said, taking the tablet and signing for the shipment and intentionally failing to make eye contact again.

"No problem," Calvin said retrieving the tablet and walking out the same way he came in, without a goodbye or making additional eye contact with anyone.

Oliver was there and completely noticed that there was a huge moment of non-verbal communication between the two of them.

"What was that?" Oliver asked, arms folded across his chest and easily identifiable as in his feelings.

Gabby dropped a looked of being completely unimpressed with whatever he was saying and shook her head.

"What, Oliver?"

She glared at him, perhaps daring him to answer in a manner that proved his obvious jealousy.

"Wow! You still like this guy!" he said in full disbelief. "After everything, you still like him?"

"Okay, Oliver, let's just assume for the sake of argument that I do – what exactly does that have to do with you? Oh!"

She quickly interjected. "And Lynne and Lola?"

Oliver first dropped his hands by his side, then placed them in his pockets.

"You know that my situation is different, Gabby."

Gabby laughed in disbelief.

"Wow," she said.

Again, shaking her head.

"I am not going to do this with you. And you know what else?" She asked.

"What?"

Oliver was becoming fully emotional.

"You and I are not going to have an argument every time Calvin shows up. I told you he was coming. Now he is back. Until he gives *ME* a reason for that to change, he will be coming here regularly! Do you understand?"

She took a deep breath and a backward step away from him.

"I guess I do understand," he said.

Oliver was pensive for a moment. He really did not like this at all.

"What do you want me to do?" Oliver quietly asked.

He was sincere. He wanted to know.

"Do you want me to leave her? Do you want me to leave my family? What do you want me to do?" He needed to know.

"I am not even sure why you are asking me that! We both know that is not an option. You have made that crystal clear" Gabby reminded him.

"You know maybe I should be asking you, what do you want me to do?" She asked in return.

"I want you to give me a chance. I want you to help me figure this out. I told you, I love you," he said

He took a step toward her but stopped shy of reaching her.

"I hear that, but it just does not sit right with me," she said.

"Oh, but Calvin does?! I saw the way you looked at him! What are you doing? Have you completely forgotten what happened with this guy?"

Oliver raised his voice, he felt himself losing it.

"I don't want you with him, Gabby. I don't see any good there!"

"But you see good in my waiting for whatever you decide as a married man, so you can keep both me and your wife?" she asked matter of factly.

"Dude! You've got the wrong person. You have really got this whole thing twisted! I am not the one!" she said.

"Do you love me?" Oliver asked, again quietly and slowly walked closer to her, then repeated the question with his hand on her chin forcing her to make eye contact with him.

"Do you love me?" he asked.

"I care about you. But I cannot say that it is love."

She felt her heart soften.

"It's something," she said, then pulled away before possibly finding herself deep in his arms – she did not want that.

He tried to pull her back to him, but she resisted.

"I'm sorry. I never wanted to hurt you."

His tone quieter and finding a true and honest part of himself.

"I love you."

"Dude. I don't need that right now."

"I need you," he said.

He meant it.

Gabby looked in his eyes. Moved closer to him, while maintaining eye contact. She put her flat open right hand on his chest, pushed him back and shook her head.

Two volunteers walked in at the very moment she opened her mouth to speak.

She stepped back.

"Just cook, Oliver," she said and headed to her office while giving morning greetings to the volunteers.

Chapter 6

(Once Bitten – Kevin)

"So, baby, are you okay?" I asked.

I did not know what to say to Kevin. We were about to cook our Thanksgiving meal, I damaged him last night, apparently badly and I didn't know if he is going to be completely incapacitated or for how long.

"What do you mean?" he asked.

He knew exactly what I meant.

"Baby, your thing… is it okay?" I asked giving a little head (no pun intended!) nod in the direction of it.

"Baby," he said, trying to make it mean far less. "It's okay."

Then he chuckled a bit.

I walked over. I wanted to touch it, maybe a gentle caress to make it better – he jumped so quickly sticking his bum out to immediately deny me access.

"Whoa!!!" he said quickly and swatted away my hand.

"What are you doing?"

"Baby," I said "I want to make it better!"

I whined a little to try to play on his love to let me touch him. "Can I touch it?"

"No! Nope! The only thing that can make it better is to be left alone!" he exclaimed.

"Until when?" I asked still hoping for access sooner rather than later.

"I will let you know."

He walked to the refrigerator, removed the Cornish hens, placed them in the sink and started removing the packaging.

"Are you angry with me?" I asked.

I was concerned.

He turned, looked at me.

"No, baby. Not at all. I just need to heal. Really, baby" he said.

"Okay," I said. I understood.

"In the meantime," he suggested, "get some tips, YouTube, Google, talk to your girls! That is, if you want to do it."

"Why can't you teach me?" I asked. "I don't know if I want to do those things."

"You want *me* to teach you?" he asked.

I nodded.

"Teach *you* how to give me head?"

I nodded.

"I can't teach you how to give head!"

He seemed to not get it.

"You know what you like!" I insisted.

"I like not being bitten or your teeth scraping it up!"

Shaking my head, I said, "You make it sound top secret or something! I want to do it the way you want it done. I am not interested in what any other person does or likes! I want you to teach me, baby!"

"Okay. Okay, baby. We can try but I don't know how to teach you. The things you did at first were amazing. I think just open your mouth wider!"

He thought that was funny and laughed out loud.

He let me get close, but not too close. He then kissed me on my forehead.

That is pretty much how our Thanksgiving Day went. While the meal was amazing, Kevin was careful not to let me get too close to his damaged thang and I was busy protecting my neck every time he walked up from behind to kiss me!

I know, a match made in heaven!

(Greta/Cameron)

Greta and Cameron had volunteered at The Kitchen on Thanksgiving Day. It helped take their minds off whatever the upcoming results would be from the MFM specialist, Dr Jordan, but they also liked giving back, even in the smallest ways.

The day came and went. There was surprisingly little communication between the close friends, Greta and Gabby, while they served together. Their lives were not clear enough in their own minds to share with anyone else. They worked together and feigned joy while encouraging and serving the largest ever Thanksgiving Day lunch and dinner.

Then suddenly, it was Monday…

(Calvin/Gabby – Feelings)

"Hello."
"Hey."
"Hey."

Brief pause.

"What do you want, Calvin?" Gabby asked.

"You looked at me on Thanksgiving Day."

"And," she asked to show the insignificance of the look.

"And I don't know. I want to tell you something," he said.

Gabby expelled a deep audible sigh.

"What (distinctively pronouncing the T)? What is it, Calvin?"

"I feel you. I know I have made a mess of everything," he said quietly and honestly. *"And I know maybe, you don't want to hear this. But I feel you, Gabby. I feel you all through my soul, like life moving in me. I feel you…"*

He waited for her to say something… and waited.

She waited too.

Then finally Gabby asked, "Calvin, what do you want me to do with that?"

"Honestly," he said *"I do not know."* He cautiously admitted.

"Then why tell me?" she inquired.

"Just like before, you don't have any idea of what you want or are willing to do. You just want to fuck something up! Bye, Calvin!"

But she did not hang up.

He noticed.

"I'm sorry. I really am," he said from the deepest point in his heart where truth lives and grows. *"I am so, so sorry. For everything. I wish I knew how to make it better."*

"Just leave me alone outside of work. That will make it better. Can you do that? And can you not call me at 6:30 in the morning when you already know I have to be at The Kitchen for a delivery from *you*?"

"Yes, I can. I just wanted to touch base with you before I came this morning. I needed to. In case you wanted me to stay in the truck," he said. *"Do you want me to stay in the truck?"*

"No, Calvin. Do be ridiculous!"

"Gabby, I'm sorry."

He needed her to hear it again.

"See you later, Calvin."

This time Gabby hung up. But she thought of him. Something about him still moved her. That same thing that made him the first man to touch her since Travis's death and gave her a desire to want to live and love again. That thing. It was still there, much to her surprise *and* dismay. Feelings were still there.

And then there was Oliver. He would, for sure be in an unnecessarily rude mood today because of Calvin.

She got out of bed and walked into the bathroom. She looked in her mirror and said to herself, "Let's see how *this* works out!"

(The Plan)

Oliver arrived at The Kitchen at 6 a.m. He knew it was delivery Monday. He knew Calvin would be there. He wanted to have the conversation that he believed Calvin was avoiding.

As he turned the lights on and opened The Kitchen, he went over in his mind how to approach Calvin without alerting Gabby to the conversation. He would wait and catch him as soon as he arrived, close the back doors and just say what needed to be said.

"Yeah. That has got to work. I am not ignoring him the way she is! I don't care," he said aloud while washing the steel tables in the back. "He needs to know that I am not playing games with him."

Chapter 7

(The Baby)

The suspense of the weekend was over. Greta and Cameron's Monday morning visit with the MFM specialist hung over them like a dark cloud the entire time. Then suddenly they found themselves sitting in Dr K'Sennia Jordan's office fully engulfed in tears.

"What is it called again?" Greta asked, almost unable to speak.

"Gastroschisis."

"And what is it again? I really could not hear what you were saying, please."

She started audibly sobbing.

"Gastroschisis. It is an abdominal wall defect; the anterior abdomen did not close properly allowing the intestines to protrude outside your baby's body. For some unknown reason, while the foetus is developing, the muscles of the abdominal wall do not form correctly. This allows some of the organs, stomach, intestine – to protrude outside the foetus's body. Your baby's intestines are outside of his body and are floating in the amniotic fluid."

Dr Jordan took a breath.

"It has progressed significantly since the first sonogram. We will need to do serial sonograms to know the severity and to find if we need to consider some more aggressive options."

Cameron attempted to be stronger than he was. He raised his head and using a controlled tone, despite his teary eyes inquired, "What are more aggressive options?"

"Well," Dr Jordan said, "there is a possibility, quite unlikely – but a possibility that the intestine could become strangulated, causing a blockage and perhaps causing some of the bowel to become endangered and perhaps fail or create problems once he is born. In which case we would consider in utero surgical intervention. But we are certainly not at that point right now."

Cameron summarised in his mind, then said,

"He has Down's Syndrome and Gastroschisis. Is that all that you found?"

"So far."

Dr Jordan quickly added, "Not that we expect to find anything else. But understand that we are continuously looking and looking very closely for anything out of the ordinary."

Quiet overtook the room.

Greta broke the silence.

"Was it me, Dr Jordan?" she asked quietly and dejectedly.

"Did I do something wrong? Is it my fault?"

She dropped her face into her hands and cried even before she could get an answer.

"Not at all, Greta. Not at all." Dr. Jordan assured her.

"These things happen on their own and you have absolutely zero reasons to blame yourself. No one is to blame here. Not at all. Okay?"

Quiet again in the room.

"I don't know what to do." Greta explained.

Greta had again broke the silence first looking to Cameron for the answer then immediately to her specialist.

"Dr Jordan, what do I do?"

"Great question, Greta," Dr Jordan said. "You are going to continue your prenatal care, we will, as I said monitor you and the baby with ultrasound and whatever is needed throughout and often. If things progress as they do 80% of the time, your son will be born in the hospital and placed in the Neonatal Intensive Care Unit. Your son will have surgery soon after he is born and stable enough to place his intestines where they belong. That is the best-case scenario. I want you to know that most of the time that is what happens."

She paused. No response from either of the parents.

"And that is all I want you to think about right now. Okay? Both of you. But I am also giving you the names of some support groups. You can decide which will likely be beneficial to you. But I strongly encourage you to start attending some support group as soon as possible. Make some calls today."

Dr Jordan passed numerous pamphlets to Greta, but Cameron intercepted them.

(A backdoor Chat)

Oliver heard the truck when it arrived. He immediately stopped prepping and went to the back door. He found himself standing on the loading dock while Calvin positioned the truck to unload the delivery.

As soon as the truck was in position and shut off, Oliver left the dock, went to the front of the truck on the driver's side and then said to Calvin, "I think we need to talk."

Calvin knew this moment was inevitable. He was ready.

"Okay."

Calvin exited the truck telling Rick to start unloading it. He and Oliver walked to the front of the truck. He waited for Oliver to start.

Oliver folded his arms across his chest, held his head high in the air.

"Why are you back?"

Calvin checked his own demeanour. He was ready for the conversation, but he felt anxiety creeping into his chest.

"Okay." Calvin said.

Shaking his head and looking away then back to Oliver he said, "I'm working."

"What else?" Oliver demanded.

Oliver's piercing eyes were not his intent from the beginning – but he could not help it.

"What do you want here? Is this the only job you can find?"

Calvin had to reach deep inside and find the control he needed. He took a deep breath and made the best peace offering he had in him.

"I got no beef with you, man."

"Really!!!"

Oliver did not believe it at all.

"Even with everything that happened?"

"Look, man, maybe it was supposed to happen. It is done now. Over. I got no beef with you." Calvin informed him. Oliver moved a half step closer to him.

"And what do you have with Gabby?"

"That's none of your business," Calvin said stepping back, while offering a significant look of his own.

He wanted to be peaceful, but he had his limits.

"How do you *know* that it's none of my business?" Oliver taunted, not backing down, His arms clinched a bit tighter in the fold.

A brief pause occurred between the two men. Time to absorb what was happening.

Calvin let out an awkward laugh.

"I'm just here for the job, man. She is all yours."

He then walked past Oliver and moved one of the boxes to the loading dock.

Oliver stood at the front of the truck a few extra moments, then helped unload the morning delivery.

Once he had taken the last box in and stored away, Calvin could not wait to get out of there. He just wanted to get the receipt signed and get out. As soon as he looked up, he came face to face with Gabby. Both felt movement in their hearts and could not ignore seeing into the soul of the other, as their eyes met and held for a couple of heartbeats. He could say nothing.

Gabby managed a noticeably quiet 'Hello'.

He passed her the tablet to sign.

When she passed it back, he did not look at her.

"Enjoy your day."

And just like that, he was out.

Oliver, of course had been there for their moment. And seemingly could not wait to say something.

"You really have feelings for him, don't you?" he asked.

"Don't start, Oliver."

She warned him.

"I'm asking you a question. That's all," he said with simplicity. "I am not asking you *not* to have feelings for him. I am just asking you to admit it."

"Dude!" I don't have to admit anything to you!"

Gabby raised her voice.

"I am not going to have an argument with you every time he comes here, and I am not going to stop him from coming. Do you understand? And I'm *definitely* not going to keep repeating this to you!"

"Really?"

"Oliver, whatever we had, or thought we had, ended the day you told me you were married and never leaving your wife. And truth is, that is not what I want anyway!"

"So, you are saying there is no way we will be together?" he asked.

"That is exactly what I'm saying, Oliver. That's what I've been saying over and over to you!" she said. "And maybe you should think about whether you want to be here or not under those circumstances."

"You're kicking me out for him?"

"It's not about *him,* Oliver. It is about what happened between us. I don't want to be that person. And I'm not going to keep having this conversation with you!"

"So, you don't love me anymore? Just like that, everything we went through together means absolutely nothing to you."

"That's not true at all," she said. "I guess I cannot expect you to understand. But I can never forget what you did for me. Never. But something in me changed when this thing with Lynne happened. And I know we can never go back."

"Yes, but I see the way you look at him. It is different than before. Deeper. Tell me the truth, are you seeing him again?"

"No, Oliver, I am not."

"Then what is going on between you two? I can see it, Gabby! Just tell me the truth. I deserve that!"

"The truth, Oliver, is I don't owe you anything, not an explanation, nothing." She informed him.

"But also," she said "the truth is I don't know what it is. There was always something there and I don't know. I really don't know. But yes, I have these strong, weird, crazy feelings for him. I don't know what they are yet though. But it's something."

"He's different. I see it. Something about him has changed." Oliver admitted that even he had noticed the difference.

"But I love you and we, you and I, are going to figure this thing out, okay?" He added.

He moved to embrace her, but she stepped aside and evaded his attempt. She shook her head and went to her office, closing the door once she was inside.

Chapter 8

(God Works in Mysterious Ways)

Greta was not ready to call the support groups and she was not ready to talk about it with Cameron anymore. She wanted to forget all of it. She wanted to believe that she had a healthy baby. She wanted the family, the dream with Cameron – for both of their sakes.

They had both cried. For days now. In her mind it was time to find the good and move forward. And while she knew calling the support groups was an excellent choice and something she would eventually do; she was not ready. She already had a support group of her own and it was time to bring them in. She would meet with her girls and figure it out.

Time was so critical right now, just weeks before Christmas. This had always been the trio's favourite time of year. Maybe the festive nature of the season would make it easier for her to uphold her full intent to no longer cry. When she heard the horn blow, she did not hesitate to scamper out of the apartment, after setting the alarm.

"What's up Gs?" she said stepping in and propelling herself into the front seat of my black Range Rover.

She was cheerful and ready for the outing.

"No!" I said. "What is up with *you*? We have not heard from you in days. Then suddenly you were ready to go out! Are you good, girl?"

Gabby reached from the back seat and touched Greta on the shoulder.

"You know," Greta answered. "I would be lying if I said I was good. I'm not. But I'm ready. I'm ready to do this."

I started the vehicle and began to drive.

"Do you want to share yet? You want to talk about what happened with the specialist?" I asked.

Gabby gave Greta's shoulder a bit of a squeeze again. And Greta looked back at her.

"The baby has Down's Syndrome as well as Gastroschisis," Greta said.

"I am sorry to hear that," I said.

"What is Gastro – you know – what is that?" Gabby asked.

"My baby's intestine is outside of his body and kind of floating around in the amniotic fluid right now."

She held her head high as she explained. She said that she would no longer cry. She meant it.

"Jesus." Gabby blurted before she realised she was saying her thoughts out loud.

"I am sorry, Greta. I'm so sorry, G." Gabby said.

Head still high Greta responded, "No, guys, there is nothing to be sorry for. I got this. It's what we have right now. And I love this baby. I love my husband. The Gastroschisis will be watched closely by my doctors and repaired once the baby is born and stable. I know children with Down's Syndrome and that is not something that will affect us and the love our family has. In fact, that will amplify it. I know that."

There was quiet in the vehicle.

"Look, guys," Greta said. "I don't need you to feel sorry for me. I need you to be here for me like Gs, my girls –

uplifting and laughing. Let us find the joy, okay? This is what I need, or I know I cannot do it (she shook her head as despair approached). I am so worried about Cam."

(She felt herself begin to sink). She quickly shook it off, stuck out her chin.

"I know we are going to be alright. I trust God. I trust His plan – whatever it is."

She took a big deep breath, laughed then said, "Now, Gs, what is going on in *your* lives?"

I cannot tell these girls what I did to my man's penis! They will never let me live it down! I cannot. So, I waited for Gabby to spill. I knew she had issues!

"I think I have big feeling for Calvin," Gabby semi whispered.

"Wait, what?" I asked.

"Do I need to pull over to hear this?"

I laughed.

"I'm serious. There's something about him that gets me."

Greta let out a 'Wow!' and we both looked at each other.

"Okay… continue…" I suggested.

"We were really great at first. But I think I was so devastated by the first night that we had together. I just wanted to hurt him by not talking to him. Then with the Herpes thing… everything got all out of hand. And Oliver swooped in like a bird of prey!"

Greta and I looked at each other again, our eyes big and our mouths stretched!

"I guess I don't really mean that," Gabby said, her demeanour failing. "Oliver was there for me at the most critical time in my life since Travis. It made a huge difference.

And he made me feel loved, valuable, unspoiled, even though, even though we both knew I might have Herpes."

She paused.

"Never mind. I don't want to talk about it right now…"

Vehicular quietness again.

Dammit!!! Am I going to have to out myself again!? Geeze! Okay let me figure out how to say it.

"So, uh… I gave the dude some head the other night."

I said this as though it was nothing significant.

Now why did both Gs, who are in obvious and considerable distress, have a brief moment of silence to digest what I said then immediately start laughing? Really?

"You know what," I said, "I'm not telling y'all anything!"

I turned the music up, held my chin high and just stopped talking.

They kept laughing.

"I'm going to turn this car around in a minute!"

I threatened them.

"G, you can't just blurt out that you 'gave *the* dude some head' and expect us not to respond!" Gabby said. "That crap is funny!"

Still laughing.

"No." Greta interjected. "It's okay. Tell us. No more laughing. Okay?" She held her face seriously ready to support and hear me out. "Tell us about it."

"No," I said. "You guys are not going to do right! I know it!"

"Come on, G!" Greta said.

Gabby added, "For goodness sake! It can't be that bad!"

"Well, (deep sigh), he actually stopped me from doing it."

"Wait! What? Why?" they asked in unison.

"Wow!" I exclaimed. "In stereo sound now?"

"Yes!!!" They both shouted again, in unison.

"Maybe I was biting him or scraping him up with my teeth," I said completely focusing on the road ahead of me.

For a moment – not a sound from the two. Then I looked at them and the roar of laughter seemingly shook the car!

Gabby first.

"What the hell?"

Still laughing!

"You cut the man's penis up with your teeth! Girl!" Greta asked. "You don't know how to give head?"

Still laughing.

"I thought I did," I said. "I thought it was going to be good. I had visualised myself making him feel all kinds of crazy ecstasy!"

Still laughing, my two best friends on this planet were still laughing at my pain. Go figure.

"Look I wanted to make him feel extraordinarily good. But I don't know, he was weird like squirming and jumping a little bit. I really thought it was so good to him at first. But he tapped my shoulder after a while and told me it was not going to happen. He said he was not going to cum. So, I stopped, I got up," I said with a small hunch of my shoulders and keeping my eyes on the road.

"What the actual hell? He stopped you?"

Gabby needed the repeat. Her laughter became uncontrollable!

"Yes, Gabby," I said. "He tapped out."

More and more laughter.

"You guys are laughing! I didn't want to hurt him! I was trying to relieve him!"

"And he told you that you hurt him, bit him or whatever?" Greta asked.

"Well, the next morning, he was in the bathroom and said 'ouch' and made sounds like he was in pain. I went to see what was wrong and asked. Then he told me that I had '*bit the hell out of him*'!"

I laughed a little. This might be funny after all.

"Oh, my goodness!"

They were both laughing so heartily and saying things related to the craziness of the situation that they finally began to make me laugh too.

Before long we were all laughing so hard that we had tears of joy.

God works in mysterious ways.

Chapter 9

(Cameron)

When Cameron saw Stassi coming through the restaurant doors, a complete feel of relief overcame him. She was not only his sister, but perhaps the one consistent supportive individual he had had his entire life. He was waiting for her at the hostess stand when she arrived and after a quick verbal greeting and hug, they went into his office.

"What is up with you, Cam?" she asked.

"Are you okay?"

"Yes," he answered quickly, initially as though the question was ridiculous.

They both sat.

"No. I am not okay." He painfully admitted. "And I need to talk about it."

"Okay." Stassi was all ears. "What's wrong?

"My baby. There are some *things* wrong with my baby."

"What do you mean?" she further inquired.

Cameron went on to explain everything that he understood from the MFM specialist. He choked multiple times but fought back tears and got it all out.

"I'm so sorry, Cam," Stassi said.

She walked over and gave him a chair hug.

Then repeated, "I am so sorry, brother. How is Greta?"

"A little weird."

He was somewhat pensive as his spoke; he did not fully understand.

"She is unusual suddenly. She had been crying a lot. Well, we both had. But suddenly, she is not. She is maybe, happier and even excited. I don't know."

He began to twist his wedding ring as it rested on his finger.

"I don't know if she cares about the baby anymore."

"Cam!" Stassi shot back quickly as though she needed to jolt him back to reality. "Cam, that is by far, the stupidest thing you have ever, ever said. And you've said a lot of stupid things!"

"I cannot tell if she cares. She doesn't really talk about it anymore. I just feel like I am dying inside, and she is nonchalant," he explained.

"She is not nonchalant, Cam," Stassi replied. "Listen. If you think that she is carrying this baby, with the issues you have just explained me, testing twice weekly for more complications and is nonchalant? Cam! Are you out of your mind?"

"She doesn't act like there are complications. She does not act like this is high risk. She laughs. She is enjoying her life." He added.

"What is *wrong* with you?" Stassi asked as she felt herself becoming angry with him. Then added, "How can you understand what you are going through in all of this, but not understand what your wife, the woman who has the baby inside of her body is going through? What the hell, Cameron?"

"I guess I should have known that you would not understand. Never mind."

Cameron shied away.

"No! Not never mind, Cam! Get a hold of yourself! Your thoughts are off!" Stassi said.

He looked at her.

"How do you know that? How do you know that I am wrong? How do you know? Has she talked to you about it?"

"No."

"You, see?"

"Cam, even you are just now talking to me about it! And you know Greta has her girls. I would not expect to be the first person she comes to."

Stassi's phone rang.

She looks at her phone, then looked at Cameron, eyes wide with an almost I told you so expression.

"It's your wife."

"Hello… I'm good. How are you? Sure, I got a minute. What is up? Yes. Oh… okay… I am sorry. Yes, he told me. Oh? Yes… you may be right. Sure… I understand. I know it must be '*Excruciating*' (she focused on the word to show Cam that it was Greta's word)… oh… okay. Yes, absolutely I will do that. I will do that today in fact. Do you need anything?"

"Just for Cameron to be okay (she repeated Greta's words and shook her head at Cameron). But you must take care of yourself too. It is about more than the baby and Cameron." Stassi continued.

"No, I understand, I get that they are the two most important things on the planet to you. I get it. Yes. Hey, thanks for calling. Sure. I will. I will let you know. Take care, babe. Talk to you later."

Stassi looked at Cameron.

"Do you feel like an ass right now? She is protecting you! She is pretending to be okay for you!"

"Is that what she said?"

"Yes! Dummy!!!"

"I don't know what to do. I got scared. I got into my own head. I always mess things up, you know."

"You are not going to mess this up," she assured him. "You are going to handle this more amazingly than you can even imagine right now. Do you know why?"

"Why?"

His eyes searching her for the answer.

"Because like everything else, we are going to handle it together."

She reminded him, "And you are going to stay out of your head, stay supportive of whatever your wife needs to do with this situation AND you are going to start AA meetings again. I will go with you if you need me to."

Cameron wiped the tears from his eyes before they came full flow.

"Is that okay?" Stassi asked requiring an answer.

"Yep. Yep, it is. Thanks, Sis."

(Calvin/Gabby – Maybe We Can Try Again)

Calvin found that he thought more and more about Gabby. He felt a connection to her that he had never felt to anyone before in his life. And it was only getting stronger. He could not get her eyes out of his head. He could not get her heart to release his. It was as though he could feel her soul attached to his. It was as though she loved him too. Even though on some level, he knew that it was not possible.

He was completely taken aback when the phone rang, and it was Gabby calling. He had to regroup his entire frame of mind.

"Hey," he said hoping she could not hear the desire for her in his voice.

"Hey," she said. *"Are you busy?"*

"No. Not at all. What's up?"

"I don't know," she answered softly. *"I needed to talk to you."*

"I'm here. What's wrong?" he asked genuinely concerned.

"I was with Greta, well, you haven't met her, but I may have told you about her before."

"One of your best friends, right?" he remembered.

"Yes."

She let out a tiny laugh of approval.

"You remembered?"

"I remember everything about you," he said without hesitation.

"Well, she's pregnant and the baby has serious complications. I just left her. She is trying to be strong, but it is tearing me up inside for her." She confided in him.

"I am sorry, bae," he said softly. "Is there anything I can do? Is she married or is the father available?"

"Yes. Cameron. He is there and he is a good man. She is worried about him though," she said, is some bit of disbelief.

"That's really great to hear. And the fact that she has you as a friend is going to be a huge part of her handling this. You are so amazing. Such an incredible part of what people on this planet needs. She's lucky to have you," he said.

"Yes, when I'm around her I can fake it. But I think it is affecting me as much as it's affecting her. I don't know if I am doing the right thing for her." She confessed.

Listen, if you are being led by your heart, you are doing the right thing. And with what I see in you, you are going to give it all you have." He added.

"Why do you see so much good in me?" Gabby asked.
She needed to hear the answer.
"Because it's the things that I have been looking for all of my life. It is very easy to recognise."
The was a pause.
Calvin apologised.
"I am sorry. Was I wrong to say that?" he asked.
"I don't know." She responded.

"You know what, Gabby?"
"What?"
"In all truthfulness, I'm not sorry. I want to tell you that and more."

He again confessed, "it's what I've been looking for all of my life".

Quiet again.

"You know what else?" he asked.

"What?"

"While I am at it, I am going to tell you something I have wanted to tell you for, well, forever."

"Okay," she said.

"It is as though the first time I saw you (pause)... everything that I had ever wanted I truly saw in your eyes. Even now, just moments before you called, even though you were not here, I was lost in your eyes. I could see them see me, and it moved me like nothing before. It was as though, everything about my life made sense because it brought me here to you. And all the pain and the disappointments that made up my past did not matter anymore. All that mattered was you. But I did not know how to do it right. So, well, you know what happened. But what you may not know is that I love you," he paused for a moment then added. "I think that's what they call burying the lead."

"I have no idea of what to say right now." Gabby admitted

"That's okay," he said. "I didn't expect you to. I didn't expect you to call me, but I'm so glad that you did!"

"You make things better, Calvin. You always did. We always had long and amazing conversations."

"Yeah. I agree. We could have been great. My fault." He admitted.

"Well, maybe not all your fault." She could finally admit.

"Truth is I was punishing you for the night you came over. I felt like trash, used, like I didn't matter to you at all."

"What?" He asked.

He was truly surprised.

"Are you kidding me?"

"Not at all." She quickly informed him, *"You did you and then left immediately."*

"I had promised my mum. Well, I call her my mum. And I went directly there when I left you. I told you that!"

"But I did not believe you, Cal. Not at all. I just felt used."

The sadness was easily recognised still in her voice.

"I am sorry, baby. But you got it all wrong."

He informed her.

"I promise you. And I did everything to get to you, but you would not talk to me. I never wanted to give up on us. Never. That is why things went so far. You completely shut me out. I didn't know what to do."

"Yes," she quickly replied, *"but you took it to a whole other level!"*

"I know." Calvin admitted. "I know I did. And I regret that more than you can possibly know. But maybe, Gabby, maybe we are over that. Maybe, just maybe we can try again."

"Hmmmmm. Yes," she said pensively. *"Maybe."*

Chapter 10

(Giselle/Kevin)

I had been practicing holding my mouth open wider and wrapping my lips around my teeth or guarding my teeth with my lips – I do not know how to describe it. But you know, so I would be sure not to bite him, scrape him or scratch him, damage him again. I had bought a cucumber that was about the size of Kevin's, well, his thing – and I practiced some licking and other things. I was determined to do it better, so while he healed, I got ready as much as possible. Well, almost as much as possible. I did not look it up on the internet at all. Anything can happen in your life, and suddenly you must explain fellatio being in your computer history! And then, everyone knows you bit your boyfriend up while trying to please him. I just don't need that in my life right now. Okay, again I digress.

So, Kevin had healed. He told me that much yesterday, but I was still not allowed to touch it – at least that's what he said. I was hoping that I would have touching privileges reinstated by this weekend. He will be back home from the fire station in a few minutes. He said he was coming over. I am trying to figure out how I am going to approach it. I wish he would ask me if I wanted to, but sadly, I am certain that is not going to happen! How can I do this?

Dammit!!! I was not able to work it in to a conversation during dinner and neither did he. We talked about Greta, Cameron and the baby. But no appropriate Segway presented itself.

As we dressed for bed, I put on my red camisole and matching panties, I always wanted to wear it for him, but instead, I always wore loose pyjama bottoms and a tank top – my usual comfort level. Tonight, I have a little something sexy on, hopefully to get his attention.

Kevin was already in bed when I came out of the bathroom.

"What are you wearing tonight?" he asked.

"I don't know. Something a little different," I said with a little flare of seductiveness. "You like?"

Smiling he said, "Of course, I like."

I got into bed with him and snuggled up to him. I did not attempt to touch without his permission, but I did reach up and kiss him. He kissed me back so – well, so passionately, so long, so deliciously – that I swear, I think I had an orgasm just from the kiss.

"Baby, are you ready to teach me?" I proposed in almost a whisper.

"Babe," he said, "I truly do not know how to tell you to do it. Do what you were doing at first. Just don't bite me or scrape me with your teeth!"

"Tell me if I hurt you," I said.

"Are you sure, Gis, that you want to try this again?" he was shaking his head.

Maybe changing his mind to not let me try it again.

"Because I'm not too sure," he informed me.

"Babe, I'm absolutely positive," I said. "Please let me try. If I mess up, I will never ask again. But you need to tell me if I hurt you, that way I can do better."

"Okay, baby. Okay. But I have a condition," he said.

I was afraid to ask about the condition he had put in place. Maybe he had prepared himself for this event beforehand. But what could it be?

I sort of squeaked out. "What is the condition, baby?"

"I want to do you first," he said and kissed me again while guiding me to my back with him on top of me.

I did not know how to respond. Was I even ready? I still don't know if I can even accept it inside of me. I didn't try that dildo yet.

"Baby, wait," I said and asked him. "Why?"

"What do you mean 'Why'?" he asked.

"That doesn't make sense to me. I want to make you feel good too. This is about both of us."

"I know that, baby," I said.

"So, if you want to do me, I have to do you first. Okay?"

He looked into my eyes and kissed me again.

"Are you ready? I want you. I want to go to the next level with you. Is that okay?"

I wanted that very much. But I wasn't sure if I was prepared in my own mind to do all of that.

"G? Baby?" He continued, "Can we do this?"

I could feel how hard he was against me. And I was hot as fire. But what if we cannot stop at oral? What if he wants it from behind? What if he sees my neck?

"I want you, baby. I want you now," he whispered. He began to move his body against mine very slowly.

Jesus.

I may have had an orgasm from that, I don't even know. More than 15 years of nothing? My body was in full explosion mode. Every touch from this man was like Fourth of July fireworks going through every bit of my body. It was good, and I needed it... oh yeah, I thought to myself, this is going to happen.

"Okay," I whispered. "Yes, baby."

(Much, much later)

I am not going to go through step for step what happened that night. But for me, it would suffice to say two things. Number one – DAAAYYYUUUMMMMM! And number 2 – he did not tap out!

(Calvin/Gabby)

Calvin's life had never been one of tapping out. He never gave up and never quit. He was a man! He was a strong man. Crafted to be so by his life. But he knew he had to change – to grow. He knew completely that he was fully in love with Gabby. But he also knew that there was something between her and Oliver that he was not interested in being a part of.

While he and Gabby spoke daily with amazing conversations, they had not spent time alone and more importantly they had not discussed her relationship with Oliver. Calvin knew that this was a mandatory conversation between the two of them. With another Monday rapidly approaching, he decided to initiate it. But he wanted to do it in person. He needed to gauge her responses, words, demeanour and vibe. He decided to ask her to dinner. Calvin loved Cajun food and decided to take her to his favourite place a Cajun restaurant simply called *New Orleans Style*. It was just a little hole in the wall place, not fancy, a bit pricey but worth it. They could have gotten carry out, but he opted for the ambiance of the place and the ability to resist the urge to make love to her.

They went through simple pleasantries while waiting for hors d'oeuvres to arrive. They discussed Greta. Just things to keep them occupied and ready to get to the gator tail bites and a couple of small salads.

They held hands across the table through Grace and looked at each other before letting go to start their dinner.

"I was a little surprised, Calvin." Gabby started. "That you were ready to get together."

"Really?" he asked. "Why?"

Gabby stopped and interlocked her fingers, elbows on the table.

"It has seemed like you felt better on the phone or maybe you are avoiding us getting together."

"Oh," he said.

Gabby laughed.

"Are you hesitant about us being alone together?" She asked.

"You are pretty perceptive." He admitted. "But we are here because I want to talk to you face to face about something. Before we move to anything deeper."

"Okay." She inquired, "What is it?"

"Here's the thing, Gabby." He prefaced the conversation. "I need you to be fully honest with me. I don't want to become more invested in you and find that I am in an unbelievably bad situation with somebody else."

"Okay." Her curiosity peaked.

"Gabby, I want to talk about your relationship with Oliver," he said.

"Okay."

"I don't really know how to start or what to ask. But the way he has always been towards me, I know there is something there. Am I correct?"

"Honestly, Calvin, yes."

"Okay. What do I need to know?"

He really did not want sordid details. Only the basics.

"I don't know where to start." Gabby said.

She confessed. "He always showed an interest in me, in my well-being. And he warned me that you were not serious about us. From the first time he saw you, he and I had a disagreement about you."

Calvin made a deep sign. "Wow. Okay."

"But he seemed to be protective of me," she explained.

"Protecting you from me?" Calvin asked almost in disbelief.

"Yes," she said.

"I'm going to stop right here, just for a minute."

Calvin needed a fresh new breath to keep his cool and absorb whatever this was going to be.

He again took a deep breath. He looked at her, then looked away – first down, then around the restaurant – as though there were answers somewhere to prevent him from losing his temper.

"Gabby, I want you to tell me everything I need to know. Everything. Then I never ever want to talk about this guy again. Okay?"

"Okay. Look, I already knew that we needed to have this conversation. I have been trying to find the perfect timing myself," she said.

She looked at him directly. She had nothing to hide, and she wanted him completely at ease, as well as protected.

"I know things have been unusual and we are working through a lot of things." Calvin admitted. "I just don't want someone else to be the reason we don't make it."

He paused then said, "Go ahead."

"Oliver and I always had this weird relationship. But he is amazing at his job, and he has made this incredible difference at The Kitchen, there is no denying that," she said.

She stopped to breathe, then continued.

"He was there for me at one of the worst periods in my life, when you told me I had herpes. To me, Calvin, that took away all my hopes for any current or future relationships. It put me in one of the saddest places I had ever been, in my entire life."

She tears up, but quickly takes her napkin and wipes the corners of her eyes, then regroups.

"I hated you. I hated you because you made me want to live and to love again. But not only did you take that away, but you ruined my hope for any future, with what you said to me."

Calvin interrupted. "I am so sorry for that." "I know I can never take that back. But know that I was so hurt too. I was wrong. *I was wrong.* I hope you can forgive me."

She laughed a little.

"I have already forgiven you for that. And I've learned a lot about Herpes and its treatment. It would not have been the end of the world. So there you have it."

They looked at each other and both smiled a little bit.

Calvin shook his head.

"Okay, baby, continue," he said.

"Oliver knew something was wrong," she said, "and was persistent until I told him. Then he was there for me, through that entire incredible devastation. He promised that life and love still existed for me, even if I did have herpes. At some point after I found out that I was negative and did not have it we became much closer. And before you ask, yes, we have been intimate."

Calvin, with both elbows on the table, interlocked his fingers and rested his forehead on his hands.

"Dammit." He knew it.

Gabby chose not to say another word until he looked up again and saw her eyes. She wanted to place comfort in his eyes through hers. She needed to protect him. And she tried.

"Oddly enough, I recently found out that he was married. I broke everything off. But I still need him at The Kitchen."

"Did he accept the break-up or is he trying to get you back?"

"He says he wants me back, but he also says that he is never leaving his wife. Which does not matter because I am not that person. I don't want him or any man like that. Fact is I don't want him at all."

She reached across the table and took his hands.

"And I am going to need you to believe that. Because you will need to be able to trust me for this to work," she stressed.

"I believe you. Is there more?"

That's the basics," she said. "I do not love him. I never loved him. But he did serve a purpose in my life and unfortunately, he still does. My chef. But that's it."

There was quiet at the table. Then the main course arrived. When the server left neither lifted a fork. Gabby had to ask him.

"Do you think you can live with that?"

"I will," he said. "I will live with that."

Chapter 11

(Cameron/Greta)

Cameron was surprised to arrive home from work and find Greta dressed to go out.

"Are you going somewhere?" he inquired.

"WE," she said, "are going somewhere."

She was smiling, cheerful almost elated.

"And where are we going?"

He was not impressed with the idea at all.

"Babe, get dressed! It's a surprise!" she said still elated.

"Babe, I am really not in the mood to go anywhere. Just tell me, okay?"

He sat on the sofa and waited for her response.

"Cam, Daniel Cross is at the Comedy House. We have tickets. We have middle section 3rd row, Platinum, meet the comedian after the show tickets! For tonight."

"Baby," She pleaded.

Cameron was considering saying no. But after careful consideration, stood to his feet, walked over and gave her a big hug.

"Okay. How much time do I have?"

"Plenty. We are the 10:30 show. Thought you might like a fast-food meal before we go. Something delicious and comforting tonight. Like a crispy fried beef and bean burrito with chili on the side. Everything relaxed tonight. Well except Comedy House dress code!"

"I like that babe," he said.

He held on a little longer, so did she. She began to feel emotional and they both held on a little tighter.

He leant back, looked into her eyes and smiled. He kissed her and then went to shower.

Daniel Cross was perhaps the funniest man on the planet. Both Greta and Cameron loved his quirky routines, immaculate timing and perfect delivery. And of course, he did not disappoint. They both laughed, sometimes uncontrollably. The Meet and Greet was almost as funny as the show itself. The man just had a way about himself that blessed everyone in his presence, in fact, the world (As I always tend to digress – I wholeheartedly believe that comedians are the most extraordinary and mandated people on the planet. What they can do to even the saddest heart, is miraculous. Proverbs 17:22 – {A merry heart does the spirit, soul and body good like medicine.}).

When they made it home, they were able to share a greater closeness than they had in weeks.

(The News)

I was so elated at work. My glow was all over the place. We had a crazy full O.R. schedule and were running behind. Surgeons were angry at *me*. Not at the other *surgeons* for running over, but at me because I was the manager.

The day was crazy, and I was as happy as I could possibly be.

Then the call came to my cell phone from Gabby.

What does she want? She knows I am at work. I pray Greta is Okay! I sneaked to my office and returned the call.

"Hey. What's up?" I asked.

She was serious from the start.

"Listen have you heard the news?

"No. What news?"

"*The* News! The actual News!"

"No! What is it?"

"Three firefighters were injured when the roof caved in at a 4-alarm fire," she explained. "Have you talked to Kevin?"

"No," I said weakly. "What hospital are they going to?"

"Yours." She quickly added, "They may already be there."

"What is the condition of the firefighters?" I quietly inquired while on the inside I was a complete wreck.

"One critical. The other two with smoke inhalation," she said.

"Look, I have to go. Thanks, G."

I hung up the phone, somehow. I called Kevin but he did not answer. I was shaking so bad that I could not remember the number to the emergency department and dialled it three times before I connected.

The unit secretary was unable to provide any information at the time. I had to do something totally out of character and against my ethical behaviour. I went to check for myself.

Much to my dismay, Kevin was indeed one of the three firefighters brought in. He however, had gone in with the second firefighter to rescue the third, who was in critical condition. As soon as I observed him from the opening to his bay, life re-entered my body. I could breathe again. He was okay. He looked at me and I saw an *'I'm okay'* smile. Thank God!

Before I made it to his bedside, however – I heard a familiar voice.

"I'm his wife! And I want to see him now! Please don't make me act a fool in here!"

Yes. It was the lovely, crazy, belligerent, will fight anybody – Michelle, the ex-wife! How in hell did she get here so quickly? How did she know he was here? Are they still together? What the…"

I overheard the staff trying to calm her and explain to her that there was a protocol in place, and she could not simply walk in to see him. And most importantly, he had to approve her visit.

"Woman!" Michelle shouted. "You better do whatever you need to do! But one way or another, I am seeing my husband!"

"Ma'am, please have a seat. I will let him know myself that you are here. Just give me a few minutes. What's your name?"

"Michelle Harper! You know? Like Kevin Harper!!!"

I leant against the wall. He had clearly heard the same thing I did. I was not going anywhere.

The unit clerk walked in.

"Mr Harper, I believe your wife is here. Michelle Harper? She is asking, well demanding to see you."

He looked at me. We had yet to touch, utter a word or in any way verbally acknowledge each other, my presence or my relief. But he looked at me first. Then back to the unit clerk.

"Thanks, but I don't have a wife, she is my ex-wife. Tell her I'm fine and I will call her right now."

He immediately reached for his cell phone while looking at me and called her.

I could hear her answer from the hall as well as from the phone in his bay – it was like surround sound, for goodness' sake! I did not move a muscle.

"Hey, listen. Thanks for coming. I am completely okay. I will be leaving soon I believe," he said while he maintained eye contact with me. I liked that.

"They just want to observe me and check my blood gases again."

"I want to see you. I need to see you Kev."

She spoke with urgency and true need to assure herself that he was okay.

('Hmph! Kev! Okay. I hear this', I thought to myself.)

"Look, do me a favour. Go home. I will call you when I am released." He offered. "Alright?"

"I want to see you, Kev."

She pleaded.

"Michelle, I will call you. Please go home" he pleaded.

"You better call me, Kevin! I am not playing with you!"
"I will."

He hung up.

There was no more noise from the outside.

"Are you coming any closer?" He asked looking at me in an anticipatory manner.

I was ambivalent. But walked over to him and sat on his gurney next to him. He pulled down his 100% rebreather mask and kissed me.

"Seeing you made me better," he said.

"Okay," I said.

I really could not say much more. Two astonishing shocks inside of ten minutes!

"I have to go back to work."

"Can I call you when I am discharged?"

"Of course."

"I love you," he said just as I started to stand.

He reached out and gave my hand a gentle squeeze.

I looked at him.

"I love you too. I swear it."

I went back to the chaos of my unit. But not the same. Dammit!

This was clearly all my fault. I had not asked about Michelle. I was fully aware of her existence, but I chose not to care. I just didn't want to be that person, jealous of the ex-wife. And he did not volunteer. So here we are. Well one thing for certain, she does not get much of his time, because he spends all of that with me. I think her checking on him was normal, but not the way she did it. And while I was disturbed by this, I was happier that he was okay. Also, he was going to need to call her in front of me!

Chapter 12

(Greta's News)

At Greta's routine bi-weekly Ultrasound, she was informed that her blood pressure was higher than usual.

"Is that a bad sign? Or does it just happen sometimes?" Greta asked, she was already on edge.

Dr Jordan explained.

"It does happen from time to time so there are some things that we are going to do. Starting with your diet."

Greta listened. But she did not hear. Cameron did not attend with her for the first time, because of a meeting he could not reschedule.

Something in her gut sank. She had dreamed of Bridget a couple nights before. Bridget was holding her hand telling her not to cry. So, what does this mean? She told no one of her dream. Yet her fear was rising at an incredible rate of speed.

"And have you started the support group yet?"

"Not yet." Greta confessed.

"Is there anything specific that you are waiting for?" Dr Jordan inquired.

"I don't know. I think maybe the longer I wait the less real it is." She again confessed. "Maybe after the holidays."

"Greta, listen to me."

Dr Jordan put the probe to the Ultrasound aside, looked directly at her and said, "I know this is hard. And I get that you want to live in denial for a little longer. But your stress is likely manifesting itself physically now. You must change some things. Do you understand that?"

She touched Greta's hand.

"The support groups really help."

Greta was interested in holding to her word that she would no longer cry. She felt herself weakening. But was able to grasp it and regain her strength.

"I will consider it, doc. But you know, I feel so helpless. It's almost like why try?"

"That's the reason you need the support groups. They help you to understand on a different level that you can't do alone." Dr Jordan replied.

"Now I have to tell Cam bad news."

"It's not necessarily bad news. It is a sign that we need to watch you closer and change some things."

"Nice spin, doc," Greta said.

"No spin, Greta. Just reality" Dr Jordan replied. "Now. Let us get started."

The entire drive home, Greta gave thought of what exactly to tell Cam. When he called, she told him everything was fine. Truth was, nothing was fine. Not only was her blood pressure up but the baby had shown no growth for two visits in a row now.

How can she possibly tell this to Cameron?

Greta really missed Bridget. It was no surprise really that she dreamed of her and the wisdom, the comfort she so frequently provided.

She again told herself she was not going to cry. She held her head up high and kept her eyes on the road. But she had difficulty seeing, the tears had a mind of their own.

(Gabby/Oliver)

Gabby sat in her office torn between this weird elation about Calvin and the madness with Oliver.

She was hurt, because she felt betrayed by Oliver, but at the same time, not only did he help through that crucial period brought on by her not so smart decisions with Calvin. But also, she had played a role in choosing not to know what the real deal was with him and Lynne.

If only Oliver would stop pursuing her, just do his job. That would make things so much easier.

They needed to talk. Seriously talk.

She pressed the intercom button to the prep space in the rear.

"Oliver, Are you there?"

"Yes," he answered.

"Will you come to the office when you get a chance?"

"Be right there. Give me five."

"Thanks."

Oliver tapped lightly on the door, then opened it.

"Hey, boss. What's up?"

"Come in," she said. "Sit."

"Am I fired?"

"No, crazy! You are not fired!"

She gave a slight laugh and shook her head.

"I want to talk."

He sat up straight in the chair from his previously slumped position and spoke a quiet 'Okay'.

Gabby changed her somewhat distant and distracted demeanour to giving him her undivided attention.

She started with this.

"I don't know if I can ever repay you for what you have done for me. I don't know, you may have saved my life."

"Come on, you know how I fee..." Gabby cut him off mid-sentence.

"Oliver, I need to say some things, okay? Then you can respond, but I really want to get this out."

"Fair enough," he said nodding in agreement and go ahead.

Gabby took a deep breath and started again.

"I know I can never repay you. And I believe you when say that you love me."

"I do love you." He added quickly.

She dropped her shoulders and gave a non-threatening stare.

"Dude!"

"Okay, okay! But I do love you."

"Oliver, I'm going to need you to be serious or let's forget it."

Oliver returned to a listening and more serious posture.

"At one point I thought that I loved you too. I learned that the expense of loving you was far too great. It was costing me my self-respect as well as prompting me to do something that as a woman I refuse to do to another woman. I am not that person. And I would never want to be."

She paused and took a sip of tea.

"I need you here," she said. "You are amazing. You've really helped make this place exactly as our vision was all those years ago. And your salary is not enough to prove that to you, I know. But, Oliver, I need you to accept that there is nothing between us. I need you to accept that you are extremely valuable part of everything that is The Kitchen. But not my personal life. That part of us is completely done, it's completely over."

"Can I speak now?"

She nodded, yes.

"I want to know if this is about Calvin."

"You didn't hear anything I just said, did you?"

She was shaking her head.

"I heard everything you said! But I have a question," he said. "Is that okay?"

Gabby thought for a second.

"You know, we have to address that too. Now is just as good a time as any. No, it is not completely about him. But yes, partially. I am tired of arguing with you when he comes here. I've told you that he will be coming. That is not likely to change, because TS and Bella love him and wants him here – mainly. I did not create the situation that brought him back. But I have come to terms with it. You must do the same thing. Much like I have come to terms with the fact that you are a married man, and we have no future. You get it?"

"I get it…" he said quiet and lacklustre. "Yeah, sure I get it."

"No, you do not! If you did your demeanour, your reaction would be different."

"I love you, Gabby."

"You have got to stop saying that! It's not good for either of us," she told him.

"Because you don't love me anymore. I don't matter to you anymore," he said.

"You will always matter to me. But on a different level."

She added, "And I need you here. I want you here. But I cannot go on like this. It is too much for me. Do you understand?"

Oliver leant his chair back on the two back legs.

"Got it, boss!"

"Come on, Oliver?"

Gabby pleaded.

"Clean slate, Okay?"

Oliver hesitated briefly but believed that the writing was on the wall. Gabby needed this change.

"Clean slate, Gabby." He sat his chair back on all fours. "May I leave now?"

"Leave now" she said shaking her head.

Chapter 13

(Fighting Fire With Fire)

Kevin's oxygen saturation, blood gases and breathing were perfect. His lung sounds, clear to auscultation. His sensorium was crystal clear, and he showed no residual effects from the smoke inhalation. I brought him home and put him in my bed, much to his dismay. But I needed him to rest. I needed him to be well. I needed to take care of him. So, I decided to take a couple days off work to be sure that whatever he required was at his fingertips.

"What do you want to eat?" I was still thinking about Michelle's antics in the emergency department.

But I had decided not to mention it.

"I don't know yet."

I was standing at the bedroom door and he beckoned for me to come to him.

"Lay here with me," he said, "that's all I need right now. You here beside me."

I did just that and nestled myself under his arm with my hand on his chest. He held me closer.

"This is exactly what I need. No food. No drink. Just you."

I lay there. Almost in complete peace. But you know I kept thinking about Michelle. I was going to see how long I could avoid bringing it up.

He sighed heavily and said, "Let's talk about it."

Was he reading my mind? Did he know I was thinking about *her*?

"Talk about what?" I whispered.

"Come on. I think I know you well enough to know that you are unhappy right now," he said, "and I do not want it to just sit there and grow. Ask me everything that you want to know about the whole situation."

"Kev, just rest, okay?"

"I cannot rest until we do this."

He manipulated his head to look directly at me. Then raised my chin causing me to look at him.

"Let's talk. Because as quiet as you were in the car, I know you cannot take it! So, let us get it all out."

I sat up in the bed and faced him.

"Okay. You tell me. What is going on? Are you still seeing her?"

"No. I'm not," he said quickly and with finality.

"Well, that may not make sense to me. Not the way she was behaving today," I said. "She was ready to do damage if she did not see you."

"She was my wife for years, Gis. And she thought I may be in real trouble, life threatening. I can understand that. I mean, I want *her* to be okay. Not that I would do the same thing she did, but I would want to know that she was okay." He admitted.

"Okay. To be honest, I understand that part. But I want to ask you something." I said.

"Ask away," he said.

"Kevin, how often do you see her? Are you guys trying to be friends or something?"

I needed to know, but I hated to ask. Seems somewhat insecure. I am not insecure; I just need to know when or if I might need to fight! She has been extremely aggressive and threatening to me. I needed to be forewarned.

"No, we are not friends. We are exes. I do not hate her. I just do not want to be with her anymore. And not only do I not see her often, but I also do not see her at all. I do not talk to her on the phone or in person. Yet, I did not delete her as a contact. Actually, she and I have not talked since she followed you home and I had a profoundly serious conversation with her. She understood. Any other questions?"

He was ready.

So was I.

"Are you going to call her and tell her how you are?"

"I promised that I would, and I am a man of my word. So yes."

"Okay" I said.

I think I wanted him to say no.

"I understand (*I understood but I didn't like it really*)."

"Are you ready for me to call her?" he asked.

"You mean you haven't called her yet?"

I was happily surprised at the question, but because I was hoping this was the case, I really was not surprised at all!

"Of course not. I saw you today. I was not making a move until we were together, even if she had called me back."

He chuckled a bit.

"Are you ready? I want to do it and get it over with."

"Okay."

I was ready for sure.

Michelle answered very quickly. He had her on speakerphone, but in a way, I was hoping he could just leave a message and never respond to her again. Sorry, just true.

"Kevin, how are you? Are you home?" She asked.

The concern in her voice was almost heart-breaking to me and for me. There will always be that bond.

"Yes. And I am perfectly fine. Thanks for checking on me." He answered.

"I had to," she said. "I care about you."

"Michelle, I really do appreciate that and everything."

He paused.

"Listen, I called you because I promised that I would," he said. "Really, thank you, thank you for caring and thank you for checking on me. Really."

"You know I will always check on you and I will always care about you," she said. "And whatever you need, just say it."

"I don't need anything. But thanks. Listen, I don't want to go backwards here. So, thanks again and take care of yourself. Good-bye."

He waited for her response.

She disconnected the call without further comment or goodbye.

She was angry. A price I may have to pay. I might have to fight later, I thought to myself... I could tell.

But not tonight. Tonight, I am going to take care of this man.

(Calvin/Gabby and The Waterfront)
Calvin wanted to see Gabby. He wanted to see her in an intimate session. He wanted to talk to her, but he wanted to

hold her in his arms. It was so important to him to not rush things. He did not want to pressure the progress they had made. So, he needed to think of some way to see her without scaring her away or making her feel he was coming on too strong.

He called her.

"Hey. I was thinking about driving to the Waterfront, maybe walking around the shops and grabbing a bite. Freezing a little bit. You interested?"

Gabby was pleasantly surprised.

"Yeah. Definitely."

"I will be by in about forty-five minutes. Okay?"

"Great!"

Calvin was a jazz man. The alto saxophone moving through the speakers of his well-kept but not stylish or new pick-up truck – moved through Gabby's soul like magic. Whether it was slow and seductive, moderate and moving or fast and furious – the music moved her soul on every level.

"Jazz man, huh?" she asked.

She smiled as she spoke.

"Jazz man."

He nodded in agreement and returned the smile.

"Sometimes," he said, "just sometimes, lyrics are not required to make a point or strengthen the spirit. Sometimes all you need is to feel the mood and let the music speak its own language."

"Oh! You're all deep, I see!" She laughed.

She continued quite amused.

"Sometimes!" he said.

He too was fully amused.

"Alright, Cal, is *sometimes* going to be your word for the night?"

"Maybe!"

He laughed.

Gabby playfully reached over and lightly hit his hand as it rested on the gear stick. He took her hand and immediately interlocked fingers, and they began to hold hands.

That felt good. They both felt good.

When they arrived at the Waterfront, Calvin parked just a bit further out to give he and Gabby a bit of a walk there and back. More time together.

Gabby opened her own door, but Calvin met her there and they instantly held hands as they walked.

It felt like *home*.

About fifteen or twenty feet into the walk, they stopped walking. They looked at each other as though to verify this reality. They first embraced, then kissed.

Yes, they were home. Finally.

Walking along the boardwalk hand in hand. Gabby laughed aloud.

Calvin was intrigued.

"What's funny?"

She looked at him and flashed a huge smile.

"Can you believe we are here right now?"

He shook his head.

"No. Never in a million years. I knew it was over," he said. "I knew I had ruined it."

"*We,*" she said. "It wasn't just you alone. I thought about it a lot. I was wrong to treat you the way that I did. I really should have talked to you about that night (she stopped walking and pulled his hand to make him do the same)."

"I'm sorry," she said looking him directly in his eyes. "I was wrong. Forgive me?"

"Come on," he said with a chuckle, "nothing to forgive."

He gave her a quick kiss and continued their walk.

Walking past the shops, a cool breeze off the water – something like a movie. Calvin suddenly stopped and looked behind them and then back at Gabby.

"We have to go back," he said.

"What's wrong?"

Gabby was perplexed. She thought everything was perfect.

"Come."

He took her hand and led her back, then into *The Best Little Toy Shop.*

"What are you doing?"

Must be a birthday present or something for a kid.

"Come. Trust me," he said and gave a small boyish grin.

They walked past rows of toys and games, to the back of the store. There were tons of stuffed animals, small to huge. Calvin found the perfect snow white, fluffy eared, oversized, bunny with a large yellow bow draped down its chest. Calvin removed it from the wall and passed it to Gabby.

There was a three-way hug and kiss with the bunny in arm. Calvin paid for the stuffed animal then they continued their walk and talk.

They ended up at a taco stand and Calvin bumped her shoulder with his and said, "Tacos? You hungry? With a frozen lemonade. It's not too cold yet right?"

"Not at all!"

Gabby laughed.

Crazy as it seemed to her at the time, Tacos sounded amazing! They stood in line together then found a table inside for the three of them.

"You know I remember every conversation we've ever had." Calvin volunteered.

"Really?"

"Yes. It's amazing the things that you remember when you are missing someone."

"What do you remember most about me?" Gabby asked in her investigative but jovial voice.

Calvin's mind sprinted to the one-time moment of intimacy and smiled broadly.

"Not that!" Gabby laughed and shook her head.

Calvin's initial laughter turned into seriousness when he said, "The devastation it brought to your life to lose Travis. And how you never allowed it to stop you."

"That was devastating." She quickly agreed.

"But I believe everything happens for a reason. I believe you are I were meant to be sitting here together, right now. I think the universe had always planned for us. Our paths were always meant to not just cross but intertwine." Calvin confessed.

"Jesus, Calvin!"

Gabby was reeling in amazement.

"Who says that? Not you! I would never take you for a universe acting on our behalf type guy! You always surprise me!"

She continued laughing, but loved this about him.

"I want to do more than that. I want to surprise you every day. I want to be what you need for the rest of our lives. I think I know that even now" he added.

"You *think* you know that? she asked.

"I do. I think that I know that is what I want, I think" (he gave what he had just said some thought). "But I know that I want to find out if it is what I want, what we want together, and I want to give everything to make it happen."

"I believe I want the same thing," she said.

As they sat eating tacos, Gabby started laughing aloud again.

Calvin looked at her mid bite.

"What *is* funny?" he asked.

Then continued to follow through with the bite.

"You love tacos, huh?" Gabby asked him, still laughing.

"I do."

Then he thought about it and asked, "But why do you say that? How do you know?"

She continued to laugh.

"Man, you've got taco bits all over your face!"

Gabby half stood and leaned over the tiny table between them, picked bits of food and wiped the residue from his face.

Calvin grabbed her hand before she could retrieve it, pulled her forward and kissed her.

They both smiled as she sat.

"At least I know what to cook for you next time!"

They both laughed.

"I know what to cook for you and *Callie.*"

She pointed to her floppy eared bunny sitting with them.

"Callie?" he asked.

"Yes."

She answered with a smile.

"She's named after her dad."

Chapter 14

(Cameron's Enlightenment)

Greta had stopped by the pharmacy on the way home and purchased a sphygmomanometer, the type that did not require a stethoscope, to check her blood pressure. The reading was digital, so checking it would be effortless. She had hidden it in the bathroom from Cameron and had chosen not to tell him that she, herself was having complications. She was recording her blood pressure daily and practicing relaxation techniques in hopes of decreasing her current measurement and reducing the likelihood of requiring medication. Her return appointment was in a couple of days, bright and early in the morning. She was hoping to show even minor improvement, it did not have to be significant. Just improvement.

But the size of the baby had her so worried. And she could do nothing about that, eating more and in an extremely healthy manner, taking prenatal vitamins and supplements were the only things at her disposal. And this was just another thing she did not want to tell Cam.

She went to the bathroom to prepare for bed, checked and recorded her blood pressure and it had increased from the day prior. She knew that she needed to be relaxed when she took the measurement and that was impossible as long as she was hiding it from Cam.

She sat on the toilet and dropped her head.

"How can I tell you this?"

She began to cry.

Cameron was already in the bedroom and thought he heard a whimper.

"Hey, babe?" he called out.

"Are you okay?"

He walked to the bathroom and the door was locked. He strongly began to jiggle the doorknob.

"Babe!"

"Okay, I'm coming."

But she could not stop crying.

When she opened the door, her face was covered with tears, and she felt crushed in her soul. So did he.

"Baby, what?"

Cam was devastated that she was crying.

He quickly embraced her and asked again, "Baby what's wrong?"

She felt herself sink to the floor and Cameron followed her.

"Cam, I need to tell you something" she confessed still crying and completely in a weakened state.

Cameron was in shock, every worst-case scenario imaginable was going through his mind.

Greta said, "Baby, I'm not well. I'm developing complications. My blood pressure is elevated, and it may be getting worse."

Cameron picked her up from the floor and carried her to the bed. He sat next to her after gently placing her in a lying position. But he did not know what to say.

After gathering his thoughts, he passed her a box of tissues and said, "Baby tell me what's going on."

She wiped her face and blew her nose, then took two more tissues from the box. She looked at him and could only shake her head.

"When you asked me how the appointment went with Dr Jordan, I lied. It was not good baby. I'm sorry, I didn't know how to tell you, but I think I have to."

"Tell me, baby" Cameron begged.

"There's a couple of things that I am going to tell you. And I need you to be okay because I need you to help me deal with this."

"Baby."

He paused and quietened himself.

"Baby, tell me what's going on."

"Apparently, my blood pressure has not been consistent since our pregnancy began. But it has not been elevated to appoint of concern. Dr Jordan says it was concerning on the last visit and gave me some things to do to hopefully control it without medications. Part of what I had to do was monitor my blood pressure myself. And I have been trying to do that. But I am supposed to be able to be relaxed when I take it and I can't. Hiding all of this from you, I'm not relaxed at all, and my blood pressure is going up, still."

"I'm sorry, baby."

Cameron felt deep sorrow but did not want to show it.

"I should have been there for you. I'm so sorry." He said.

"It's not your fault, baby." Greta quickly interjected "I know how much you want this baby. And I wanted more than anything to give you a beautiful and healthy baby. But I am failing you miserably!"

She starts crying audibly.

"No! NO!" Cameron yelled at her in somewhat of an effort to startle her out of those thoughts. "Don't ever say that you failed me! You are everything that has made me want to live and be a better man. You brought me back from a place Greta, I can never repay you. And you loved me. No one has ever really loved me before you. But, baby, why could you not come to me? Why? What did I do wrong that you do not trust me?"

"Cam, it's not that at all. But I did not want to disappoint you even more. But, baby, I must – there is more, Okay?"

Cameron and Greta took deep sighs, almost in complete unison.

"The baby's weight, his growth has not increased for the past two visits."

She waited for his response.

Cameron felt his heart tear apart just a little bit in his chest. He tried to speak. He wanted to say the right thing. But he really did not understand. And in his whole soul, he knew that he should have gone to the last visit with her.

"I am so sorry, Greta. I should have been there. You should not have had to deal with all of this by yourself. I'm sorry."

"I'm sorry, baby. I just wanted to protect you," she said.

They both ended up in tears.

"We will do it all together from now on," Cam said. "Together from this day forward. We will not keep things from each other, right?"

He waited for confirmation.

"Yes, baby."
"Because, baby, we are stronger together."
He added. And they were.

Chapter 15

(And She's Really Back)

I loved watching Kevin sleep. He looked so peaceful, not as though he stared death in the face on yesterday. I could not send enough thanks to God for sparing his life. It was amazing how this man had become intertwined in my heart and soul even without knowing him for a year. And now the thought of being without him for any reason was almost unbearable. I could not imagine what this morning would be like if the outcome of performing the duty of his chosen career, had been different.

"Wait, what?"

His cell phone just received a message. Well, I was standing next to it. I really must look at it. I may need to wake him, after all.

Ahhhhhh. A message just came through from the ex-wife!

"Can we have lunch anytime soon?"

She is inviting him to lunch. Wow! And why does he NOT have a lock on his cell phone? And why does he not have it put away? There should have been some way for me *not* to have seen that message. Careless on his part!

I could not with this woman. Really? I did not really know what to do. I was pissed at that moment.

I quietly left the room.

I really felt anger and jealousy building up. I wondered if he would tell me. That was a huge consideration. If he did, it would demonstrate a trust and strong belief in our bond. If not, to me – it would demonstrate the opposite. She did not ask him to come over, rather she asked just for lunch. Well, that's something good. Okay.

I was going to have to wait this one out. I was going to behave as though I never saw the message. I would continue to nurse him back to wellness as I had taken today off to be there for and with him. What happens next is the question.

(Cameron/Greta)

Last night was incredibly difficult for both parents to be. The news of the mounting challenges with their unborn son, was almost incapacitating for Cameron and he woke running to the bathroom to vomit.

Greta woke by the movement of his rapid exit from the bed and followed him to ensure his wellness.

"Cam…" she called to him lightly, then seeing his state, she turned on the water, dampened a cloth and wiped his forehead while he leant over the commode.

"Sorry. I am good. I do not know what happened. I just woke up so nauseated. Sorry to wake you."

"Baby, that is completely okay."

She continued to wipe his brow.

"Babe, go back to bed. I am perfectly fine. It was likely what I ate last night. But you need to rest."

He stood and splashed water on his face. He took the dampened cloth from Greta and covered his entire face.

Greta stood in the door of the bathroom. She knew he was unprotected. She knew she had to be strong. For Cameron, their son and for herself.

"Hey, babe," Greta said, "can we go for a walk? Get some fresh air?"

He looked at her. He knew what she was doing. He did not want to. But he also did not know if it was a good idea.

"How about, you rest for about thirty minutes and if your blood pressure is good, we will take a short, emphasis on short, walk."

"Okay."

"In the meantime, are you hungry?" he inquired.

"No, babe. But would you just cuddle with me, hold me?"

"Ah, baby. Absolutely. Absolutely I will."

He nodded and they headed back to bed.

They found safety.

They found comfort.

They found peace.

They found relief… in each other's arm.

And they even managed to fall asleep again.

Cameron woke first. He eased out of bed and headed downstairs, ensuring to take his phone with him. His plan was to whip up a nice brunch for Greta, but he also needed to make a couple of phone calls.

"Tommy, I need you to cover for me for me today and take Greta off the schedule at least the next couple of weeks. Is that possible?"

"Yeah, man. Sure I can do that. How are things going?"

" As well as can be expected I guess. I may be able to come in later but call me if you need me for anything at all. Okay? And thanks again, Tommy."

He ended the call to Calibri's but immediately went into the next call.

"Hi."

He paused.

"I'm not good at all." He sat on the sofa and dropped his head in his hands. "I need to see you."

He raised his head to look for Greta, who was not there.

"No," he said. "I have not taken a drink. But I am feeling something, and I don't know what I'm going to do."

He paused, then added, "Sure. At 11, okay. Thanks, Noah."

Noah had been his sponsor from day one. He had seen Cam through his worst and helped him to his best. Cameron was not willing to let himself down or to let Greta down. He had grown enough to know that he needed to take control before his addiction did.

He washed strawberries and peaches, sliced them and dropped a few grapes in. Just as he began to prepare waffles, Greta walked in.

"Good morning, baby," she said.

"Babe! What are you doing up?"

She sat at the bar and looked at him with wide eyes. "I woke up and you were gone."

"Baby, I'm making you breakfast in bed! Go back to bed and rest."

She hesitated. He insisted.

"Go back to bed, rest! I need maybe five minutes and I will be back. Okay?"

He walked over and lightly kissed her on the forehead.

"Go."

"But I was thinking I could just sit here with you."

She was a little pouty and childlike in her tone.

Cameron picked her up from the bar stool and carried her back to bed kissing her between each word of "I. Want. You. To. Rest!!!"

He finished and brought waffles with whipped cream, honey and a few pecans on top, the fresh fruit and orange juice. He skipped the coffee.

He sat the serving table across her, opened her napkin, kissed her forehead again and said, "I love you so much."

"I love you too, baby."

"Listen, I've taken you off the schedule at work for a couple of weeks," he said quickly adding, "and don't argue with me. It is a done deal."

"No. I think that is a good idea."

He took a quick scan of the room then asked, "So where did hide your blood pressure machine?"

"In the bathroom, in the linen cabinet, behind the large towels on the bottom row."

"Goodness! You were seriously hiding it. We never get that low."

Cam laughed then retrieved the sphygmomanometer and Greta's record book.

"I want to check your blood pressure. So, tell me how this thing works."

Greta guided him.

"136/70."

"How is that compared to yesterday?" he asked checking the record book.

"It is lower, babe. It was 138/88 yesterday," She answered.

"We have today, then the weekend. And we will see her on Monday. I think that is okay. But if it goes above 140/90, she wants me to come in right away."

"Okay. We will check it again tonight and see how you are doing," he said. "But I need to run out for a bit. Maybe a couple of hours. You know you can call me, anytime."

He looked at her for confirmation.

"Seriously, Greta. Call me."

She laughed.

"I will."

(Sponsor Talk)

When Cameron walked into the coffee shop and saw Noah, he had to actively fight back tears.

They shook hands then embraced.

"What's going on, man?" Noah asked.

Cameron paused. He looked at Noah and waited for the lump in his throat to pass before starting the tale of complications plaguing his life right now.

"Man. My heart is with you." Noah started. "And I am really glad you called me."

"I really appreciate you meeting me, man."

"It took a lot of courage for you to make that call. I'm really proud of you, man," Noah said.

"I am determined, Noah, I will not drink again. I have not and I will not!" Cam said.

Noah slid a piece of paper to Cam.

"Here is the meeting space and times. I think it would be helpful to attend a few."

"Cam nodded.

"I agree."

He looked at Noah as though he wanted to say something else. But then turned his head away.

Noah noticed and asked him, "What is it, man? Is there something else on your mind?"

Cameron again hesitated, looking around the room.

"If it's something that's weighing heavily on your mind."

Noah added, "I encourage you to let it out. You do not have to do it right now. But at some point, you need to address it."

"I know."

Still looking around the room as though he was afraid to make eye contact. Cameron hesitated. Then he let it out.

"I keep thinking about my wife – she never wanted a child, man. Somewhere in my mind I keep thinking, somehow, it's her fault. And I know." He added, "That I think it is, somehow, my fault as well. But I feel angry with her."

"I heard what you said, and I know those thoughts must be devastating, Cameron," Noah said. "Does she have any idea of those thoughts?"

"I am not sure that she cares enough about this situation to think of what I feel or think," Cameron said. "She tried to keep some things really significant from me."

"Have you considered talking to her about how you feel?"

"I thought about it. But when I talked to my sister about some of my thoughts about it, she said I was way off base."

"But you do not think so?" Noah asked.

"I really don't," he said.

"Cameron, what exactly are you basing this on?"

Cameron breathed heavily then said, "Of course she never ever, wanted a baby. Then suddenly she was doing whatever she wanted, she was not upset – even when we got worse news, she seems to be okay with it. Then I found out she lied to me, she withheld the truth about herself and the baby. She knew I would make her do better. I cannot seem to reconcile this."

"Do you think she deserves to know these thoughts you are having? Do you think that maybe talking to her can help you to reconcile these thoughts?" Noah asked.

"I don't know." Cameron admitted.

The two men had sat and chatted for nearly an hour and a half, when Cam ended the session.

He felt better, but he knew that he needed to talk to Greta.

Chapter 16

(Crisis)

Later that evening when Cameron arrived home he found Greta in the kitchen.

"What are you doing?"

He could not hold back his displeasure and his raised voice with a teeth gnashing grind and grimace.

"Just getting a sandwich, baby. I was a little hungry." She admitted.

"Babe why didn't you call me? I told you to call me!" He exclaimed.

"I know," she said. "I just wanted a sandwich."

The trash can caught his eye. He had emptied it prior to leaving, sat the bagged trash next to it and was going to take it out back when he returned.

"Baby, where is the trash? I left it here."

"I took it out," she said.

"I was going to do that when I got home. You could not wait for me? It had to go?"

He was getting angrier by the moment.

"What are you trying to do, Greta?" His tone was harshly accusatory.

"What do you mean 'what am I trying to do', Cam?"

"Are you *trying* to lose our son?"

He was straight matter of fact. And he didn't really care.

"Cam!"

Greta was shocked.

"Did you ever really want our son?"

"Cam, wait," she said as her heart sank. "You cannot possibly know what you are saying."

"Do me a favour, Greta! Just answer me! Did you ever want a child with me? Simple, yes or no!" He yelled. "Did you ever really want our son?

Greta did not know when she started to cry, but there was suddenly a flood of tears rushing down her face.

"Why, Cam? Why are you doing this?"

She wailed.

"Do you think I haven't noticed you? Well, I have. I've noticed everything. And I know all it took for you to try to lose our baby was some complications. Then you were completely out."

"Wow," Greta said quietly.

She felt her whole body grow limp, but she did not fall. She *refused* to fall. She gathered all the strength she had in her body, straightened her posture, and held her head high. She found her keys, phone and purse, and left without another word.

Cameron watched as she walked out of the door. He was still angry, and he believed for the next five minutes, that he was right.

Then it hit him.

"What did I just do?"

(Jackass)

When I heard the doorbell ring, I was in bed snuggling with Kevin. It felt so good. I gave some thought to not answering it... but you know.

I looked through the peephole at Greta and was truly startled to see her. She did not call first. She did not even know if I was home. What could possibly be this horrible?

"Hey..." I said.

I could not get to another word because she fell into my arms crying like I had never seen her cry before. My first thought honestly was that Cameron had died. But it was even worse.

"He blames me..." she said. "He believes this is all my fault. Everything with our baby. He blames me."

I was stunned.

So, we embraced a little longer and I then led her to the sofa.

"No. Greta. That can't be right," I said. "It's not possible that he would blame you for this. Did he say that?"

"He said *EXACTLY* that!"

She looked at me in full disbelief, crying and shaking her head. She looked as though she needed me to do something magical. Something to make this all go away. I could not.

I sat next to her and said, "Tell me what happened."

Greta told me the whole story. And I was horrified. I was somewhere between finding that jackass, Cam and endlessly hugging her.

"Can I just stay here with you while I figure this out? I can't go home. I can't face him again tonight. I don't know if I can ever face him again."

"Of course, you can stay with me, G, of course."

"But I need you do more than let me stay with you. I need you to not tell anyone at all where I am. I can't talk to anyone. Not now."

She continued crying and wiping her eyes with tissues that happened to be conveniently located on the sofa table.

"Greta." I shook my head. "Do you want to *hide* from Cam? I'm not sure it's a good…"

She quickly stood, reaching for her purse and quietly uttered, "Never mind."

She had a look of complete defeat as she attempted to leave.

I took hold of her arm and immediately stopped her progress.

"Of course, you can stay here, and I swear I will not tell a soul. No one. Well, Kevin is here. But I will not tell another soul," I promised.

And there was no way I was going to break that promise. Even if I had to lie for her.

She sat. She cried. I sat with her. I cried with her.

"Thanks, G," she whispered through such a sadness that I felt it in my soul. I could do nothing. Not even joke about beating the dogshit out of Cameron.

"Anything. Anything at all, okay?" I said.

I looked at her and raised her sunken head.

"I swear, G, I got you. I swear."

And I meant it.

Later, I got the spare room ready and gave her some of my clothes to sleep in. And I prayed, with everything in me, that she would be able to sleep.

Kevin was awake when I returned to the bedroom.

"What's going on?" he asked. "I heard some pretty bad things."

He shook his head.

"Yeah, babe, I need you to not discuss it at all, okay?"

I asked in honour of my word to her.

The guys knew each other. So, I needed him in agreement from the word go.

"I gave her my word not to say that she was here. I need to keep that word."

"Not a problem," he said.

"Baby, it is not a problem right now, but I don't know how long she needs this," I said.

"Okay. No problem. I understand. Got it!"

He assured me.

Then his phone rings. He takes a quick look at it and his demeanour changes, He looks at me, then turns the phone around for me to see. *Michelle.* He tosses the phone to me. Bold, huh?

"Answer this," he said.

"Hello," I said.

"Who is this?" she sounded surprised that it was not Kevin.

"Kevin passed me the phone. He's resting," I said.

"I know who you are," she said. *"You live in the same building as he does. You are Giselle. I know who you are."*

"Okay," I said. "But he is still resting so, what do you want me to do?"

"I don't want you to do anything," she said rather matter of factly. *"Nothing at all. It's all about me now."*

"So, I'm not going to talk to you in riddles," I said "but I will tell him to get back to you if he wants to. I don't care, not at all."

She scoffed a bit.

"I'm going to have to beat your ass, huh?"

"You might have to try. Yes" I informed her. "You might just have to try." I repeated myself.

I discontinued the phone call and threw the phone hitting Kevin.

"Really?" I was a bit upset, but oddly enough, a bit satisfied that he gave me the phone.

"I guess you thought I wouldn't answer it!"

"No. I knew you would answer it!" He laughed.

"This is not funny at all, Jack!"

"Jack?" he asked.

"As in *Jackass*!!!"

He laughed!

"You need to talk to her," I said seriously. "You need to call her, tomorrow. She is talking about fighting, yet again. You know that's not who I am. At that was like a setup!"

"I will." He said. "I will talk to her. Do you need to be present?"

"No. I think that would make things worse," I said. "I just need you to resolve whatever it is. I don't want to live with this third person wreaking havoc in our lives."

"Okay."

He reached out to me.

"Come to bed."

"I don't want to come to bed right now! You are not in the best place with me at the current time!"

I hope that I do not have to fight. I'm too old for that. Especially having anything to do with a man. But if she goes too far – I will.

(Trust)

That night, Greta's dream was vivid and again Bridget.

She dreamed Bridget and she was at the beach in Africa. They sat in the cool breeze of the sunset and Bridget took her hand.

"I know you are hurting. But will you believe me if I tell you everything is going to work out?" Bridget asked.

"How can it possibly be?" Greta asked.

"Because you love God, and He loves you. All things work together for the good of those who love Him and are called according to His purpose."

Bridget answered.

"How can He love me and allow this to happen? Everything? And now Cameron?"

"He loves you. Understand that He knew this would happen before it ever did. Nothing happens without passing God's divine inspection first. He has already placed everything inside of you that you need. And He has already made a way," Bridget said. "But you have to keep the faith. Do not give up. Trust Him."

"And Cameron?"

"Cameron is struggling. He is trying to find his way without losing himself. Are you able to be there for him?"

Bridget asked again, "Are you able to be there for him?"

Suddenly Greta woke from the dream, and she cried more. Maybe what Bridget said was real.

But after what happened the answer to that question, 'Was she able to be there for him?' was *Fuck no!*

Chapter 17

(Pancakes and the Past)

Early Saturday morning when Gabby walked into The Kitchen, she saw Lynne and Lola having blueberry pancakes. She smiled at the two of them.

"Good morning," she cheerfully said.

"Good morning," said Lynne first, then Lola, who looked adorable with pancake syrup on her face and an almost unwillingness to stop eating.

Gabby smiled broadly; she was somewhat surprised to find that she was almost completely unbothered by seeing them. Almost.

Oliver returned with chocolate milk and placed it on the table near Lola. He then leant over and kissed Lynne. He managed to keep a slight visual on Gabby – just to see her reaction. He sat with them, looking toward Gabby.

"Good morning, boss!"

Gabby laughed and said, "Good morning. Great to see you guys here. What a beautiful family. Lola enjoy those pancakes!"

"I *love* blueberry pancakes!" Lola answered quickly. "Especially when my daddy makes them!"

"Your dad is an amazing cook, Sweetie. See you all later."

Gabby left the family and went to her office. She knew exactly what Oliver was doing. She just did not quite understand why. And she did care. She did not want to, but she did – just a little bit.

Not so long thereafter, Oliver was knocking on her office door. That was inevitable, he had to check on the progress of his plan.

"Hey, boss. You got a minute?"

"Are you done making blueberry pancakes?" Gabby asked.

He laughed.

"I so rarely get to cook for her. I really wanted to make her favourite food. Today is her birthday."

"Oh great! Happy birthday to her. Why didn't you say that in the first place?"

"I would have," he said, "but you left so quickly I didn't get a chance to tell you anything."

"Well, you had a mouthful going on, you didn't have much time to say anything to me." She argued.

"I kissed my wife."

"While looking at me!" She shook her head. "What was that all about? Want a little drama in your life? Or are you trying to bring drama into mine?"

"Neither," he said matter of factly. "I just kissed my wife."

Gabby wanted to reason with him.

"You are so much better than this. You know that, right? This is below you."

"Kissing my wife is below me now, Gabby?"

"Do you really think that I do not know what you are doing?"

"I believe you *think* that I am trying to make a point to you. Truth is, I am trying to get closer to my family. Like you have suggested," he explained.

Gabby felt exhausted by the entire conversation and situation.

"What do you want, Oliver? Why are you here right now?"

"Do you think I can leave early today? I want to do something special with Lola tonight, celebrate a little."

"Of course."

Gabby answered very quickly. "Just let me know when you are ready to go. Now if you would excuse me. I have a couple of things to do."

Oliver did not turn and leave, he slowly backed out instead. He closed the door behind him, but took a second look at Gabby first, who had already stopped looking at him.

(Carla Baptiste – Step Mum)

Saturday had moved fast. There was lots of work on the farm and Calvin just wanted a hot bath and to see Gabby.

As he finished up, his phone rang. He was instantly transported emotionally to New Orleans.

The call was from his best friend, Ben. They had kept in touch over the years but had not actually seen each other more than four or five times since Calvin left New Orleans just over twelve years ago.

"Ben?"

Calvin was excited to speak with his old friend.

"Man! Is that you?"

"Yeah, brother it's me!" Ben replied with the same excitement.

"How are you?"

"Man! I am great! How are you?"

Calvin was smiling from ear to ear. He had not been this elated in a long time.

"I can't believe you still have my phone number, man. It's been, I know, over a year or two, right?"

"Yeah man, but my number never changed. I was hoping that yours did not change either," Ben said. *"So, things are going well for you, huh?"*

"I guess as well as they can be nowadays."

Calvin was suddenly a bit concerned.

"What's up, man? Seems like something is on your mind."

Ben took a deep breath.

"Yeah man. Your sister, well, your half-sister asked me to call you."

"Why?"

"Man, your step mum is not doing well at all. And she is asking for you. That's all she will say to anybody – 'I must talk to Calvin. Find Calvin. I want Calvin'. Man, she is in bad shape, but she cannot rest because she wants to see you, to talk to you."

Calvin was quiet. He had not seen his stepmother Carla, since he left, nor had he spoken to her. Memories of her were not pleasant at all. He never wanted to see her again. Even if she was on her death bed.

Ben spoke up. *"You still there, man?"*

"I'm here," Calvin said with no emotion.

"Bruh, you know I know the whole story. But I felt like I had to tell you." Ben said.

He waited for a reply.

"What are you thinking, man?"

"I don't know." Calvin hesitantly responded, "the old me wants to say absolutely fucking not! But I am not that same man. Somehow, maybe I need to consider it. Is she in the hospital?"

"No, Man. She is on home hospice, terminal cancer. Man, she really does ask for you almost 24/7."

"Look, thanks for calling. I just do not know right now. But do me a favour. Send me her address. I will figure it out."

"That is easy," Ben said. *"It's your old house. She never moved."*

At the end of the conversation Calvin did not know how to feel or what to think.

Bella walked up and saw him standing in the foyer of their home looking perplexed.

"Son, what's wrong?" Bella asked fully concerned.

He trusted her.

He knew she cared about him.

He took a deep breath then told her.

"My step mum, Carla, is dying. They say she is asking for me."

"Come, let's sit."

She led him to the sofa, and they sat.

She put her hand on his knee and continued, "I can tell that you are conflicted about going."

"She hated me" he said "She made my life a living hell. But now, she wants to clear her conscious before she dies. I already know it's all about her. Not about me."

"Son, you get to make the decision as to whether you go or not. But ask yourself, are you willing to give up the last opportunity to ask her anything, anything at all? And yes, it may only be about her, but maybe consider if you will ever want to know what it is that she needs to say to you. Maybe you do not need to ask her anything. Maybe you do not need to know what she has to say. Maybe you are good. But then, maybe not. Maybe going and hearing her out can be one of the most healing things you can possibly do for yourself. Either way, if she is dying, understand that you will not get the chance again – that is if you even make it in time now."

Bella leant in and gave him a hug.

He held his head down. This was harder than he would have imagined. He looked up at Bella and confessed.

"I don't know what to do."

She smiled.

"You do not have to know at this moment, son, but I know you. It will come to you. Whatever you decide, just let us know. We are here for you. If you need us to do anything, just say the word."

They embraced again and Calvin headed to his car.

The short walk to his car and the brief conversation with Bella ensured that he knew what he was going to do. He went home, packed a bag and was ready to hit the highway, heading to New Orleans. But he needed call Gabby first.

"Hi, babe. A situation came up. I'm on my way to New Orleans."

"Calvin, what's going on? Is everything okay?"

She knew a little about Calvin's life in New Orleans. She knew that his mum died in childbirth and his dad died when he was 11. She knew he had a horrid step mum, that her name was Carla, but nothing more.

"It's Carla," he said. "She's in hospice and she is asking for me, they say continuously asking for me."

"Do you want company?" She offered.

"I'm kind of dropping everything and driving down tonight. Can you do that?"

He knew that he would love having her there with him but was uncomfortable asking.

"Have you left yet, can you come get me?" she asked. *"I just need to see if I can get things in place at The Kitchen first."*

"Okay. I will see you soon," he said. "I wanted to see you first anyway."

"Come on over. I will make it happen." She promised.

Gabby hung up and immediately called Oliver.

"Hey, were you planning on coming in tomorrow?"

"Of course. Why?" he inquired.

Something has come up and I need to be out for a few days. Can you cover The Kitchen until I get back?'

"Of course, but what's wrong, Gabby?"

He was concerned.

"I will be available by phone if you need me."

She intentionally did not answer.

"Are you okay, Gabby?"

He was concerned but not relieved.

"*Is something wrong?*"

"Thanks, Oliver. I really appreciate the concern, yes, I'm okay. I just need to do something, and I do not want to close The Kitchen on such short notice. Can you just take care of things until I return?"

"*Sure, Gabby.*"

He relented.

"*I will take care of things. But update me from time to time, okay?*"

"I will." She assured him. "Thanks, Oli."

Gabby packed a bag quickly and decided to call Bella to let her know where she would be.

Bella was slightly surprised to get the call.

"*Hi, Gabby! Are you okay?*"

"Hi, Bella, yes. I want to tell you something."

"*Okay,*" she said.

"First, I'm fine and everything is fine with me. I am going to New Orleans with Calvin tonight. He and I are friends, good friends. Truth is, I love him. And I think he loves me too. I am going with him; in case he needs me."

She waited for Bella's response.

"*That may be the best thing I've heard in years! Thank God.*"

Bella's voice was emotional as though some prayer had been answered.

"*I was praying he had someone to go with him. Now listen, I don't know if he will want it, but as soon as he told me what was going on, I chartered a private plane to take him there with whoever he wanted to accompany him and for the return trip. The plane will be available out of Shanandoah Airstrip in three hours. He does not know yet, because I just finalised the reservation and you called before I could call him. I knew he would go,"* Bella said proudly.

"Wow, you really love him, huh?" Gabby gleaned.

"Like a son." Bella said.

The doorbell rang as they spoke. When Gabby opened the door and saw Calvin, she immediately said, "Bella is on the phone," and handed it to him.

"It *is* better to fly." He acknowledged. "But do you have any idea how expensive tickets this late, if we can get them, would be?"

Gabby watched though she could not hear, she knew what Bella was saying.

Calvin was listening closely and looked to Gabby.

"I don't want you to do that," he said quietly.

"You've already done it?" he asked.

"Can you undo it?"

He began to choke up emotionally, but he shook it off, held his head back as to make it go away.

"Okay."

He surrendered. He walked away from Gabby for a bit of privacy.

"Nobody has ever done things for me like you and TS. I can never repay you. You make me feel like I really matter. Thank you."

When he was done with the phone call, he walked over to Gabby and placed the phone in her hand saying, "She chartered a private plane, a rental will be waiting for us, and we already have a hotel room. She took care of everything."

"She loves you. She told me." Gabby said.

Calvin felt ambivalent about everything surrounding the trip to New Orleans, including the fact that Bella had extravagantly made and paid all the travel expenses. He was tender inside. He was completely vulnerable.

Once they arrived in New Orleans and settled into their hotel room, he decided to share with Gabby, the details of his life that led him to leave – full details.

As she listened to him discuss how his father treated him before his death and the long line of abuse from Carla, his stepmother, to living on the streets as a teenager – she tried to just listen – but she could not help but cry.

"I'm so sorry, baby," she said shaking her head. "You never deserved that."

"I know," he said. "But it was like, I was always searching for myself, for better, for what I really did deserve – to be loved. Seemed like I never knew who I was. I never felt like I was me, like I was myself or who I was meant to be. As though I missed being something – maybe because I missed being with my mother. I don't know."

"I'm sure that's a part of it." Gabby agreed. "And the way it went with the people who were supposed to love you, that was not your fault in any way – your dad and Carla, they both were just screwed up on the inside," she said.

"I'm really glad you decided to come here though, Cal" Gabby comforted him. "I pray there's closure here. But if not, the fact that you came here for her, shows that despite what they did to you, they did not win. Because they did not harm the core of who you are right now. You are a good and decent man. I really believe that."

"Wow," he said. "Thanks for everything tonight. Thanks for coming with me."

He kissed her.

"Since we now have a bit more time, thanks to the chartered plane – I am going to shower; do you want to join me?"

"Yes," she said. "Yes, I do."

Chapter 18

(Stolen Identity)

Greta was lying on a sofa resting her head in Bridget's lap, as Bridget sat and stoked Greta's hair. Bridget said nothing, but the breeze through the patio as they looked out on the ocean was amazing. Greta felt completely relaxed. No worries. Then she started to lose the feeling. She was waking up.

Before she could completely wake up, Bridget said, "It is as it should be."

These dreams… she kept to herself.

But she woke that Sunday morning without a sense of who she was or who she had ever been. She was only certain that she no longer wanted to be the person she was a couple of days before. She had blocked Cameron and had not talked to him for more than 24 hours. She had not been on social media at all. She ordered underwear, all toiletries and change of clothes online and had it sent overnight. The only person she talked to was Giselle.

Yet, it bothered her a bit that she did not know if Cam had tried to reach her or not. But she was not ready to know that yet.

The Christmas season was heretofore, her favourite time of year. But that was no longer something that moved her. She was lost.

I was scrambling eggs when she came into the kitchen that morning.

"Morning, G," I said. "How are you?"

She sat at the bar and shook her head. No answer.

I poured then passed her a glass of orange juice. "Do you want to talk about it?" I asked.

She started to cry. Silently.

"I do not know who I am anymore," she said. "Somewhere during everything with Cam and the baby, I've completely lost me. I don't know how to think or what to think."

She continued to cry, while taking a paper towel I passed her.

I removed the eggs from the burner and sat next to her.

"What can I do, G?"

She looked at me, then her entire face went blank. She fell to the floor.

"Greta! Jesus!!!"

I tried to wake her. She was breathing, she had a pulse, but she was unconscious. I quickly called 9-1-1. I put a cool cloth on her forehead and remembered that she had a sphygmomanometer. I checked her blood pressure, and it was 248/168. Jesus!

"Greta, relax," I said.

I did not know if I could calm her or ease her stress by talking to her in an unconscious state, but I had to try.

"Greta, I swear, it is going to be okay. My God! My God please!!!"

I prayed aloud with everything in me.

The ambulance, paramedics arrived, and I told them what I knew. They worked to stabilise her and were quickly on their way.

I drove behind them and while the last person I wanted to call was Cameron, he had a right to know. I finally gave in once we reached Santana County General Hospital's emergency department.

"Cam, it's Giselle. I do not have time to talk. But Greta is at Santana County Hospital. Her blood pressure is crazy high, and she is unconscious."

I could hear him saying, *"Santana County! What?"*

"Yes, Santana County General Hospital. Emergency. She is unconscious. You better get here!!!"

And I hung up. And I did not answer him back.

I did my best to complete her registration. I had somehow gotten her purse before we left, and her ID and insurance information was there. I did not know about allergies and all. But I did the best that I could. Suddenly I remembered Gabby.

She answered in an incredibly jovial manner.

"Hey, G! What's up?"

"Hey, Gabby," I said. "Greta is in the hospital."

"What! What happened?"

Her demeanour quickly changed.

"Her blood pressure went up, she passed out."

"She what!"

"She passed out. Her blood pressure is really high." I added.

"Is she okay?" Gabby begged.

"We just got here. I don't know yet. She's in the back, and this is not my hospital. We are at Santana County; you know

I work at regional. I wish we were there; I wish I could find out something and be a bigger part of whatever happens with her treatment."

"Oh my God, Cameron must be a wreck!" Gabby said.

"Yeah, look can you come over here, like right now?" I pleaded. I really needed her support before that jackass got here. I did not know how to deal with him right then, not alone.

"G. I am so sorry," Gabby said. *"But I am in New Orleans."*

"New Orleans!" I gasped.

"It is a long story," she said, *"but we took a chartered flight last night. I am with Calvin."*

"Aw, dammit..."

I was so disappointed.

"Okay. Hey, I'm going to go, but I will call you back as soon as I know something."

As soon as we finished the conversation an extremely professional looking female in scrubs opened the door and called for Greta's family.

"I am."

I stood and walked over. I was scared to death.

"Come with me," she said.

Then the professional, looking at the door, called to Cameron, by name – who was emergently running through the doors. This must be their OB-Gyn doctor or the specialist.

Cameron could not wait and began questioning her before he had fully approached her.

"Dr Jordan, how is she? How is Greta? Is she going to be okay?"

"Cameron, come with me."

She led the way, I followed too.

We both went with the doctor to a small room just off the front desk and away from the patients.

"Cameron," she said, "this is urgent – Greta's blood pressure is dangerously high right now, and the baby is not thriving in utero. I wish I had more time to talk to you about this, but the truth is, if we do not get her in the operating room right now, we can lose both, your wife and your son. I need you to know that we are going to do everything that we can. But I cannot promise you that either of them will make it out alive. No matter what we do, we may lose them both. But if we do nothing, they both will *definitely* not make it. And we must move quickly."

Cameron shook his head as though to clear it and understand what was being said.

"What?" he was cloudy, trying to understand.

"Hear me, we are going to lose both if we do not go now. I am asking for your consent. And I am making you aware that we may lose both no matter what we do. Do you understand? But we must go now. Can I get your consent?"

"You have *my* consent!" I exclaimed almost angrily.

"Who are you?" she asked quickly.

"I am her sister, her best friend on this planet!"

Cameron could barely speak, but somehow interrupted me.

"Go, go. Yes, you have my consent."

Leaving quickly, the doctor said, "The nurse will have you sign the papers."

Cameron looked at me, a completely shattered man.

"What did I do?"

"Life happened. Now is not a time for blame. It's a time to pray," I said.

"You just don't know."

He began sobbing.

I informed him,

"As a matter of fact, *I do know*. And we both need to be praying right now. We don't have the time or luxury of blaming and feeling sorrow or whatever. So don't start crying now. Use that energy to manifest everything with grace and mercy that you can muster!"

I stood and began to exit the room, then came to a full stop. I turned back to him.

"Do you want to go to the chapel with me?"

"I have to sign the consent."

He did.

(Stolen Identity New Orleans Style)

Calvin stopped at the wire fenced gate into his step mum's home before he and Gabby went in.

"Thanks for coming with me," he said.

"It's going to be okay." She said with a slight smile.

They cautiously approached the door and rang the doorbell. Someone Calvin did not know answered the door and introduced herself as 'Amanda, Mrs Baptiste's caretaker'.

Calvin told her who he was and why he was there. She invited them in and offered them a seat. Amanda then went to the back room to inform Carla.

A few minutes later, an extremely emaciated, unbelievably small, frail woman emerged, oxygen in tow and on the arm of her caretaker. Her breathing was audible, with a notable wheeze and somewhat laboured.

"You did not have to get up for me," Calvin said.

He walked over and assisted her to sit, then returned and sat next to Gabby, who quickly took his hand.

"I don't know how much time I have left," she said.

Her breathing was more laboured as she spoke requiring several breaths between her words and sentences.

"But I had to see you. Thank you for coming."

Her voice was weak and trembling.

"I need to give you something."

She pointed to Amanda.

"Bring me the box, wrapped in brown shipping paper, on the floor in my closet. It has Calvin's name on it."

Amanda left the room.

The room was quiet.

His step mum broke the silence and said, "I treated you wrong. I am sorry. That doesn't change what I did."

She breathed shallow between breaths but kept going.

"You deserved better than what I did, better than what I gave you."

Calvin shook his head and said, "Don't worry about that. I'm okay. I've been okay."

"I see. You are a fine man" she said. "And the way she is holding on to you, almost to protect you (nodding), she really loves you. You deserve that."

"This is Gabby," Calvin said.

"Hi, Gabby. Thanks for coming here with my son. And thanks for loving him. You love him, right?" she asked.

Gabby while looking at Calvin said, "Yes I do. He's an amazing man."

She squeezed his hand even tighter. He returned the love.

Amanda emerged from the back with a large box, still sealed for delivery, but no address. Carla directed her nonverbally to give it to Calvin.

"I have said I was going to get this to you for years now. I should have," Carla said. "Open it."

Calvin opened the box. The first item inside the box and separate from everything else, was a homemade DVD, labelled 'from Dad'.

He looked at his step mum.

She pointed to the TV and said, "That DVD player works. I think you should play it now."

Calvin looked at Gabby. He held the DVD in his hand, then tapped it on his knee. He was so uncertain.

"Do this one thing for me, Calvin, please listen to it here, now."

His stepmother pleaded.

He slowly approached the dusty DVD player, discerned how it worked, turned it on and placed to disc inside. He walked back over to Gabby and sat near her, and she again took his hand. He hit play.

Calvin immediately recognised his father. He knew that it was him and memories started to rise. His father's face was the same young man he remembered as a child, but his eyes were reddened as though he had been crying.

His father began the soliloquy that would change Calvin's life forever:

"Calvin... (long pause) Calvin. I guess that is a good place to start. Calvin. Well, that was never meant to be your name. Your mother named you and called you by your name for months before you were due to be born. Your mother, (another long pause) your mother was and always will be the best thing that ever happened to me. She was always the love of my life, she was everything. When I lost her, I lost all feeling for everything in my life, yes, including you. I know that was wrong, but I tell myself, I had no control over it. I still do not know if I do or not. But without her, I no longer existed, even though you did (His father takes a drink from a whisky bottle). Calvin. Calvin – no. That is not your name. Your name is Zion Alexander Baptiste. But I could not bring myself to give you that name legally and call you that after hearing your mother say it so many times. So, I picked a random name I saw on a worker's badge at the hospital and called you Calvin. I did not even give you a middle name. Just Calvin. What I know now, is I was wrong. What I do not know is how to do better or how to fix this. And I know that I love you. I know that I do. But I do not know how to separate you from losing the best thing that ever happened to me. Every moment of my life I spend loving and missing her. I do not care who I am with or how much she loves me, I just cannot escape the pain of losing your mother. No other woman will ever have my heart. Not ever. So why am I telling you this? You are only ten years old. I don't know where my life is headed but I want you to know the truth if anything ever happens to me, I am sorry I was not a better man, a better father for you, son. I know that I do love you. I do. And you deserved a better man than me as your father. But here we are... I love you, Zion. I love you, Zion Alexander Baptiste."

The video ends.

"I was ten years old. He died a year later. I don't understand. Did he kill himself?" Calvin urgently asked.

"No." Carla answered. "He had a heart attack. A massive heart attack. And died seven months later. I found this. I was mad. Really mad! I was furious. I started to destroy it. But I couldn't."

She struggled to get the words out.

"I'm sorry."

She began a somewhat strangling cough.

"Lung cancer," she explained. "Cigarettes (Changing the subject back to the reason he was there)."

"In the box are things that belonged to your father and your mother. You do not have to open them here. Unless you want to. I just wanted to explain the truth about the DVD."

She began to cough more aggressively.

Amanda said, "You may need to lie down now, Mrs Baptiste."

Calvin removed the disc from the DVD player.

"We are going to let you rest."

He carefully put the disc back into the cover and placed it solidly into the box and closed it. He took the box, then he and Gabby readied themselves to leave.

"We will check on you tomorrow. Okay?"

She nodded.

"Thank you for coming, Calvin. I needed you to know. And Calvin," Carla reiterated "I am so sorry for everything I took from you and denied you. You always deserved better than what I gave."

Calvin did not respond. Instead, first picking up his box, he and Gabby simply turned and left. Their ride to the hotel was either quiet or superficial.

There was no mention of the box in the backseat.

Chapter 19

(Greta – In the Woods)

I was not sure if Cameron had called Stassi, so I did. He had not. I told her what was going on and asked her to come support him. I knew that no matter what happened, I could not.

We had spent a lot of time in the chapel praying but returned to the waiting room for word about Greta and the baby's condition, as soon as it was available. The three of us sat quietly waiting, when Dr Jordan returned, she again took us to the back room. I knew this was not good at all. The question was just how bad was it?

We all sat.

The first words out of Dr Jordan's mouth:

"The baby did not make it. Greta is in the ICU. She is stable but her condition is still critical. The next few hours will mean a lot. We are doing everything. All we can do now is wait."

None of us said a word.

"If I thought telling you to go home would help," Dr Jordan said. "I would. But I think you are better here."

Still not a word from any of us.

"Any questions?' she prompted us.

Cameron in a weakened state asked, "Can I see her? Can I see my wife, please?"

"Sure. I will make that happen" she said. "I will send the nurse out. She will help you.

"How long will she be in the ICU?" I asked.
"Depends, And I cannot guess. We need to make sure she is stable in multiple ways right now. And unfortunately, she is not there yet. She is not out of the woods yet."

"I understand," I said. I wanted to see her too. But I knew not to ask. She needs as little stimulation right now as possible. Trying to stabilise her is of utmost importance. Not relieving my soul's need to place eyes on her. But she needed her husband… I think.

So, Cameron was going to see her. That was the right thing, but I did not like it. Not at all. Yes. I fully blamed him. And I wanted to hurt him for hurting my friend. But I could not. I needed to be able to pray for my friend. I needed to fully manifest positive and healing energy. Not *the punch him in the nose until it bleeds,* energy!

I was in such a way from dealing with everything surrounding Greta, that I forgot there was a man in my life that I could depend on for support. My phone was on silence and checking it finally, I had missed eight phone calls from him.

"Hi, baby, I'm so sorry. Greta had an emergency. We are at Santana County."

"How's Greta?" he asked.

"She's in ICU. She lost the baby," I said. "And the doctor says she is not out of the woods yet."

"I'm sorry, babe," he said. "Is Cameron there?"
"He's here."
I really did not want to talk about him.

"If Greta doesn't make it, I will never forgive him, Kevin."

"I know, just try not to think in that direction. I'm praying with you, sending all positive energy."

He was encouraging me when I needed to ask him how he was doing.

"Do you need anything?"

"No, babe," I said. "I'm good. Oh, baby!" it hit me that I had not asked about him. "I am sorry! How are you feeling?"

He laughed.

"I'm great. I feel fantastic."

"What are you doing?" I asked.

"Well, I just had a conversation with Michelle. I think she understands. I did tell her that we were together, and I wasn't going to do anything to jeopardise that."

"Oh, Jesus!"

I was exhausted at the thought.

"She nearly jumped me two or three times before. I just know she's coming at me now that you told her that!"

"No."

He assured me.

"She promised to just leave us alone. She said she was worried about me. She needed to know I was okay. She wanted to see me. So, we had a quick lunch, and we are done now. She knows that."

"You went to lunch with her?"

"Yes," he said, "I felt that I could get through to her better in person."

"Did she talk about getting back together?"

First, he hesitated then said, "She did. And it was a good thing. I was able to make it clear that we were over. I told her to move on. I told her that I already have moved on."

"With me?"

"Yes, with you, Giselle. I am with you. We are together. I told her that," he adamantly stated.

"Dude, I know at some point she is coming after me."

"Stop saying that!" He somewhat demanded. "She is not coming after you. She has no reason whatsoever to do that!"

"Man! I hope you are right."

"Trust me, okay?" He almost whispered.

He sounded so convincing.

But I know what she put me through before and somehow, I cannot see her just letting it go.

I had been at the hospital all day and it was starting to get late. The nurse allowed us to come in one at a time at 8 p.m. and see her for a total of fifteen minutes.

Cameron told me to go in first because I had not seen her at all.

When I saw her, lying there, multiple IVs infusing, non-rebreather oxygen mask at 100%, connected to multiple machines and a beeping sound consistently chiming in the room – I almost lost it.

But instead, I held her hand. I kissed her forehead. I told her that I loved her. I told her that everything would be alright, and I prayed for her.

I straightened her blankets and did a little tidy up on her room. I stood in the door just for a second before I left just to look at her.

And I prayed some more.

I walked out and told Cameron to go in, Stassi had left earlier to pick up her children from school.

He stopped me and said, "If you need to go and do something, it's okay. I will be here all night. If anything changes, I will call you. Is that okay?"

I had not showered, and I did need to check on Kevin.

"I do need to go," I said. "But I will be back."

"Okay," he said.

Then reached out and hugged me. I gave him a hug. He really needed it.

Chapter 20

(Calvin/Zion)

When they returned to the hotel, the name Zion Alexander Baptiste, kept ringing in Calvin's head. He placed the box on the table and sat directly in front of it. Gabby stood behind him and gave him a hug.

"You okay, babe?" she asked very quietly in his right ear.

With both hands he reached up and held both of hers.

He made a deep sigh and said, "Yeah, I think so. I am just trying to absorb what just happened."

She twisted her body around his and made her lips meet his and kissed him, deeply and inviting.

He rose to his feet and accepted the invitation, walking her backwards to the bed, leading her to lie back and joining the top of her.

He needed her. He needed to be inside of her.

She knew it and she welcomed him in.

And it was as they both had always known it would be, even from the very beginning.

Finally... Gabby had fallen asleep after their session, and Calvin eased his way back to the box. He was not sure why he was hesitant. What could be more shocking than a whole other identity? He opened the box and removed the DVD again.

Then he finally said it out loud, "Zion Alexander Baptiste. Zion Alexander Baptiste. Somehow that name makes me feel more important, like I matter just a little bit more than I do as Calvin. That's crazy as hell!"

He spoke aloud to only himself.

"Wow."

He began to carefully remove the contents of the box. He first removed the sheet of white paper that separated the disc from everything else. He then visually investigated the box before removing the next item. It was arranged and labelled; the first item wrapped in a white cloth from a white envelop labelled *'This first layer belonged to your mother'*.

Apparently, Carla had prepared or had someone prepare the box and detail its contents, to give Calvin the best experience and full knowledge.

When he opened the cloth, he found a beautiful, perhaps twenty inch long, gold chain with Jesus on the crucifix. He held it in his hand and inspected it.

"Wow," he said.

He put it around his neck immediately. His eye instantly caught three small jewellery boxes. He found first, a pair of gold hoop earrings. He laughed a bit. The next box contained what appeared to be diamond stud earrings.

"Okay," he said. "Nice."

The final box had a small note *'your mother's wedding rings. I never saw them until after your father's death'*. They were so beautiful; Calvin immediately closed the jewellery box – he could not stand to look at them.

The last item on that layer was wrapped in paper and he knew it was likely a photo from the 8 x 10 size. It was a photo of his mother lying on a sofa with her head in his father's lap and his hand on her large very pregnant belly. The note inside said *'this is you'*.

"Dammit!"

He was louder than he intended or even realised that he was.

"Is something wrong?" Gabby asked.

"No. Not at all. Rest."

He looked at the photo and shook his head.

"Dammit!"

This time much lower. He was not sure whether he wanted to even investigate the next level. Everything so far had created a whirlwind of emotions and he was completely outside of his usual comfort zone.

He returned everything to the box, except his mother's crucifix – which he left around his neck. He would not see any more items tonight. But tomorrow. Yes, tomorrow.

He returned to bed and nestled himself closely to Gabby. She turned to him and embraced him. He fell asleep in her arms.

Just after he cried – a little bit.

Calvin realised somewhere in the night that he would not finish examining the contents of the box until he was home. He needed to be in familiar surrounding before any other surprise presented itself. When he woke Gabby was already up and dressed.

"Good morning," she said.

"Good morning," he answered. "I want to go back to Carla's this morning."

"Okay. Is it okay for me to go with you or do you need to go alone?" she asked.

He had tossed and turned through the night. She was not sure.

"I need you to come with me. I need you there. I always want and need you. Always."

He sprang out of bed and gave her the biggest hug then said, "Let me shower. I'm ready!"

His phone rang while he was in the shower. But Gabby did not answer it. Once he was out, she told him he had missed a call.

Calvin checked the phone and said "Hmmm. Ben. He probably wants to see us before we leave. I told him we were here."

He retrieved his 'voicemail'.

Then listening, sat slowly on the bed with his towel still wrapped around him.

"You have got to be kidding me."

He instantly made a phone call.

"Man! What?"

He paused and said, "But I was there last night. I talked to her last night! Are you sure?"

He paused again.

"Wait, what? Where? Okay, we will be right there." He hung up the phone and looked shockingly at Gabby.

"Carla died last night," he said.

Gabby gasped.

"What?"

"Yes. And she had asked to be cremated immediately. No funeral. She is at Brook's Funeral Home. The family is there. They want us to come."

Carla's two adopted daughters met Calvin and Gabby at the funeral home. Ben was engaged to her oldest daughter,

Brie. Her younger daughter Kicha, appearing in her early twenties, was quietly shaking her head, perhaps in disbelief. They all hugged as a family then sat together in chapel.

"I'm really blown away by all of this," Calvin said. "I didn't see it coming."

"She was ready to go, man. She just wanted to see you," Brie said.

"She answered a lot of questions for me. Some I did not even know that I had. It is really a lot to digest right now." he confessed.

Gabby held his hand a little tighter but did not say anything.

Ben, a bit burly in appearance but with a kind voice.

"I imagine the past twenty-four hours have been a whirlwind for you."

"Yeah, man," Calvin said. "Too much to even discuss. But enough about me, what happens now with Carla?"

Brie answered, "We have always known what she wanted. She made it pretty clear for the past year as she deteriorated. So, she was cremated overnight. They are preparing her ashes. It will only be us and a couple of her friends in about an hour. Just a little memorial. It's how she wanted it."

"Can you all stay for it?" Ben asked.

Kicha interrupted, looking at Calvin saying, "She talked about you a lot. More toward the end. She said that she wished things had been different. Then it got to where you were all that she wanted."

"There were some things that she wanted me to have and some things that she wanted me to know. I'm glad I was able to come." Calvin admitted.

"What time does your flight leave, when are you leaving?" Brie asked.

"Well, we have not really decided."

He looked at Gabby.

"But we will most likely leave today. We have to call the pilot and see how long it will take to get the flight plans."

"What the hell!" Ben said somewhat loudly and surprised.

"What does that mean, man? You got a private jet?"

"I do not." Calvin laughed. "But someone made arrangements for us, and it included a private plane."

"Whoa! Dude!"

Ben rolled back and laughed.

"Man, you got mad connections! What are you doing?"

"It's not like that! Not at all." Calvin was serious. "I'm not that person anymore."

"Okay." Ben said as if to humour him.

Ben was still laughing and certainly did not believe the change was true. He remembered the old days from the streets.

But Calvin was indeed not the same kid from the streets of New Orleans.

He and Gabby stayed for the brief memorial and flew home that evening.

(A little of Michelle's Mind)

Michelle sat in her car thinking about Kevin. She knew she had messed up. But she never believed that he would divorce her. She knew more than any other thing in her life that he loved her. And she was always the one who did the leaving in relationships. She was used to doing whatever she wanted to do. Men always allowed her freedom to be herself.

She sat there, in the parking lot of Kevin and Giselle's apartment complex as the darkness of night fully settled in. She sat, thinking and talking to herself.

"I know this is all your fault, *Giselle*! So, he does not want to be friends with me. He does not want to see me, talk to me or anything. I just know it is all because of you, bitch! I know it. I just know it."

She took a huge toke from her blunt.

"I'm going to learn your routine and his routine and when the time is right – oh *how* I am going to beat your ass!!!"

Spoken with pure ecstasy in her voice.

"It's just a matter of time!"

Chapter 21

(Grief Relenting)

Cameron had spent the night in the waiting area of the ICU. He slept relatively upright and in increments not greater than 30 minutes. His devastation at the loss of his son and the condition of his wife was only magnified by his guilt. There was no question in his mind, it was his fault.

He looked at his watch and it was 6:12 a.m. on Monday morning, when I came through the door with Starbucks and a lemon iced scone.

He took the coffee but said, "I'm not hungry," and waved away the scone.

"Eat it," I said. "When Greta wakes up, I don't want you to be weak, crying or in any way thinking about yourself. You are going to pull yourself together starting right now! You are going to be there for her. Your time to rise and be the man that you know you are, is right now! No self-pity or self-blame. What happened cannot be changed. No falling off the wagon. What's done is done! You get it?"

He dropped his head. He cried.

"I get it," he whispered.

I softened my tone and added, "Because you don't have the luxury of being weak right now. Do you want Greta to live, to be healthy?"

"Of course, I do," he said looking up teary-eyed.

"Then you must be strong. Put the past where it belongs and focus on making her believe that there is a future worth living for."

I looked him square in his eyes and added, "I am not kidding, Cam."

"I know that you are right," he said.

"And I know that this is hard. It is hard for me too."

I could not hold back the tears.

"But right now, it has to be about her."

I took a deep breath and let go.

"Have you heard anything yet?" I inquired.

"Yeah, the nurse said she had a good night. Her blood pressure has been stable, but she has developed a low-grade temperature. They are monitoring her and doing everything."

He almost cried again but looked at me a held it.

"I am not saying don't feel this Cam (noticing his restraint). And it is okay to cry, but when she sees us, we both must be together and encouraging her."

"I've never ever hurt this bad in my life," he said. "How do I do this?"

"You know. You do it. You just do it. That is the only option. You do it hurt, sad, scared, heartbroken and in the most pain you have ever experienced in your life, but you do it. For you and for your family. Not *just* for you and Greta, but your future children – your future life. That's how you do it!"

(Girl! I heard myself after I finished that pep talk and thought – 'Wow! That was good. I must have channelled some Bridget!)

Cameron stood, placed his face in both of his hands and took a deep audible sigh. When he opened his eyes, Dr Jordan was entering the ICU waiting room.

"Good morning," she said.

"Good morning," Cameron said slowly but anxiously. "Is there news?"

"Yes."

She smiled and said, "Greta did well through the night. She had a low-grade temperature, but it quickly recovered, and she has remained stable through the night. I think there is a good chance that we will move her to the floor this evening. We will know by the afternoon."

"Thank God!"

Cameron and I both gave thanks at the same time. It was a truly welcome relief.

"Can I?" He stopped and looked toward me then said, "Can *we* see her?"

"Of course, you can," she said. "At visiting hours. You have about two hours from now and you will be able to see her for fifteen minutes."

"You should go shower," I said to Cameron. "She's apparently out of the woods now. Go shower and come back. I will be here."

He briefly hesitated, then said, "Okay."

As he walked out, he stopped for a moment. Then turned back to me as though he planned to say something, said nothing and turned to leave.

He stopped again saying, "I can't believe I'm living this reality right now."

I recalled what Greta was going through before this episode, but I also could see his pain. This was not about me.

I said rather candidly, "Try not to think about that, Cam. We're all living it together and we *all* wanted so much better than what we got. But we are headed in the right direction. We just have to make the best of where we are and what we have."

(Oliver)

It was Monday morning and there was a shipment coming from the Farm. Oliver was not interested in seeing Calvin. And just the thought of it made him anxious. He was opening, getting ready for the day, when The Kitchen phone rang.

He answered quickly, "Kitchen (pause). Oh, Gabby? Hi!" he said.

Gabby: "I will be in this morning but around nine or ten, I think. Are you good with that?"

"Yeah. Of course. I will see you then," he said then quickly asked, "are you okay?"

Gabby: "Yes. I am good."

"Are you sure?"
He further inquired.
"You sound a bit off."
Gabby: "Thanks. I am good, really. See you later."
Oliver began to consider seeing Calvin there, without Gabby as a buffer.

"I'm not ready for this! I know it," he said aloud.

He called Lynne.

"Hey, babe, why don't you get dressed and you and Lola come here and let me make breakfast for you guys again?"

He paused for her answered.

"Thanks babe, get here as soon as possible, okay?"

(Thoughts of Zion)

Calvin and Gabby had stayed the night at her place. The flight back, compounded with everything that had happened in less than forty-eight hours had been exhausting for both, but most especially Calvin.

Gabby was making breakfast when he woke – the smell of bacon would not allow him to rest. In the kitchen, Gabby was slicing tomatoes, he walked behind her and kissed her neck.

"Good morning," he said.

Gabby leant her head back for a more kissable kiss on the lips.

"Morning," she said as he complied.

She stopped slicing, turned to face him and asked, "How are you?"

Calvin walked around to the table and sat.

"I keep thinking," he said, "and I know this is crazy. But what if I'd had the chance to be Zion Alexander as opposed to Calvin nobody?"

"Come on, baby, you are more than that," she said.

"I guess but hearing that did something for me. And I had never seen the picture of me in my mother's stomach."

He looked around the room and noticed that he did not bring the box in.

"I will be right back."

He returned with his box and placed it on the table.

"Why do I feel like I am a different person now? Why do I feel like I am more than what I was before I got this box?"

Gabby removed the bacon from the oven dropped bread into the toaster and pondered what to say.

Calvin continued, "I mean, I feel like a whole different person from who I was before Ben called."

Gabby removed two plates and began to put bacon on them.

"What's different to you?"

Calvin thought, then said, "I have always known that my father hated me. But I just learned that he loved me too. And I don't know how to reconcile the two things. He took his love and my identity."

The toaster popped and Gabby removed the bread. She began to scramble eggs while asking, "Do you think knowing this was a good thing or do you even know yet?"

"I feel a strange happiness, I feel that I am Zion. It fits me in my soul, my spirit. Can you understand? I was never the person I had to be as Calvin. I cannot explain it."

He was looking at the picture of his parents and himself.

"Zion Alexander Baptiste. The way my father said it, he was proud of me."

Emotions began to creep up in his chest. But he did not want it to take over.

"Wow!" he said and laughed a little bit.

Gabby brought his breakfast and juice and sat it next to his box and he went further into the contents.

Calvin laughed aloud.

"Really!"

He removed a New Orleans Saints football jersey, and several other items of Saints memorabilia.

"He was a big Saints fan. I had forgotten about that!"

He then removed a leather Saints Jacket and two watches, one wristwatch the other a chained pocket watch, that when opened contained a young and beautiful picture of his mother. Finally, he removed a bottle of Old Spice cologne.

"I will not be needing this!"

He scoffed at the cologne.

"I could probably add water to this, after all of these years and make seventeen bottles of Old Spice!"

Calvin returned all the items to the box except the photo, closed the box and sat it on the floor. He reached and held his mother's crucifix hanging around his neck.

He was quite pensive initially then stated, "I realise that my father had a lot of issues. He did not know how to cope. Maybe he did the absolute best that he could. Somehow, I guess I just turned out to be collateral damage."

He slightly shook his head.

He then looked to Gabby and said, "Thank you for being here for me. I have no idea how I would have handled all of this without you."

"Thank you for letting me be there. And I know you Calvin, you are such a strong amazing man. You would have handled it."

She placed his breakfast in front of him and they both began.

Chapter 22

(Out of the Woods)

Cameron returned to Santana County General Hospital, fresh and wide awake. I knew we were rapidly approaching visiting hours and was really excited to see her. I also knew it was right for him to go first. She was finally where she could really communicate with us. He needed to see her. It was right. I could wait.

When the nurse brought Cameron to Greta's room, he stood and looked at her briefly before fully entering. She momentarily appeared asleep, then suddenly opened her eyes, seeing him. He felt a need in his soul to run to her bedside but restrained himself and held to a relatively brisk pace. He sat next to her bedside, eased his face onto her thighs and held it there while he composed himself.

He slowly raised he head, as she was stroking it.

"I'm so sorry, baby… forgive me," he said.

"There's nothing to forgive."

She whispered.

He knew he was not supposed to cry – but he did.

"I love you. I love you. I love you."

"I love you too, Cam. And I need you to be okay about this."

"Baby, do not worry about me. Just please, baby, please be okay. We can do anything if you are okay. I promise," he said. "I will take care of us. I promise."

He placed his face back on her thighs as he spent the next ten minutes sitting with her.

She drifted off to sleep with him there and for a short moment, he did as well. But suddenly he awoke.

"I have to go get Giselle."

He looked at her, stood and kissed her forehead.

"I will see you after four hours."

"Cam, get some rest, okay?" she requested. "Do that for me."

"I will, love," he said.

I knew I only had a couple of minutes to see her. I could have punched Cameron for taking all the time, he is only a couple of inches away from a punch anyway!

But I was so happy to see her eyes. She still had oxygen by nasal cannula in her nostrils, but the nonrebreather was gone.

"Hi, G," I said.

"Hi," she said.

"I love you, girl. But you are just a little too dramatic for me!" I joked and sat on the side of the bed holding her hand.

"Take care of Cameron for me," she said.

"I am," I said. "I know you well enough to know that you would say that. I got you. Just get well. Take care of *you."*

(The Kitchen Delivery)

Travis Sr (TS) had decided to drive the truck and make the delivery himself with Rick and an extra guy, Jaxon. He backed the truck to the dock and knocked on the door.

Oliver was ready. He would not react no matter what his feelings were for Calvin. He was taken aback when he opened the door to TS. While he did not know him very well, he had met TS once or twice at The Kitchen previously.

"Good morning, sir," Oliver said.

"Good morning, uh – he was attempting to remember his name.

"Oliver."

"That's right. Oliver," TS said. "Come on, give us a hand."

Oliver went straight out to help, and they stored everything away nicely once the truck was unloaded. TS was seated in the front when Oliver came out to sign for the delivery.

"What time will Gabby be in this morning? I hear they got back really late last night," TS said.

"She said later, I'm thinking around eleven or so," Oliver guessed.

"Yeah, that was a quick trip, very emotional for both she and Calvin. I told him to take the whole day off, so I am out here making deliveries."

TS headed out the back door not noticing that Oliver was too stunned to respond.

"Tell Gabby to call me if she needs anything."

TS disappeared to the backdoor and left.

Oliver sat.

He did not know much about what was going on with Gabby's emergency time off, but what he did know was too much. He quelled his anxiety waiting for her to arrive.

He put a big smile on his face and walked over to his wife and daughter.

"Are you guys good?"

"Are you okay? Lynne asked.

"Yeah. Thanks for coming up. I just wanted to see you guys for a bit," he said. "What are you going to do for the rest of the day?"

"Going grocery shopping. Getting ready to cook Christmas dinner. Well, getting ready for you to cook it anyway!"

She laughed.

"Okay," he said and kissed Lola and then Lynne. "I will see you guys tonight."

Oliver was having so many thoughts that he wanted to scream. Additional staff/volunteers started to arrive, and he did not want anyone to say a word to him. He was unable to respond when they said good morning. He needed to keep his words until he was calm. Until he knew what to say or do.

But Gabby arrived just moments behind the volunteers. And he had no time. He wanted to keep his newly found information to himself, but his mind, mouth and tongue would not let him.

"Good morning, Oliver," she said.

"I guess it is for you," he said.

"What?"

"How was your weekend?" His question had a bite on it, and he was visibly upset.

Gabby walked past him. She was unsure about what was on his mind but was certain that she was not going to share some of the most private events in Calvin's life with him.

Oliver followed her into her office. He was somewhat relentless in his need to get to the bottom of her emotional weekend with Calvin that TS knew about.

"I heard," Oliver informed her, "that you had an emotional weekend with Calvin."

"And where did you hear that?"

"TS made the delivery this morning. He casually mentioned it."

Oliver waited for her response.

Gabby sat. She collected her thoughts. She pointed to the chair and Oliver sat. She put her elbows with her fingers interlocked on her desk. She pondered the situation.

"I do not answer to you, Oliver. Do you understand that?"

"I don't want to see you hurt again." He insisted.

"Oliver, listen to me."

She tried to think of what to say that would be of value, to the point and not hurtful.

"I would be lying if I said that I don't appreciate everything you did for me in the past. But I would also be lying if I said that I was not very hurt by what happened between us in the end (Deep sigh). Oliver, I am completely done with you. You are the chef here; I want you here. But I don't know if you really want to be here anymore. I need you out of my personal life," she pleaded with him.

"Did you marry him?" Oliver needed to know. "Just answer that for me."

Gabby said with an exhausted laugh, "No. We did not get married. But I want you to know that I really have strong feelings for him. And I think I always have."

"You still have those feelings after everything that has happened?" He asked in disbelief.

"I do," she said. "Maybe even more."

"Wow! Then I am out of it. From this moment I am completely out of it." He abruptly stood and left the office.

Gabby picked up the phone and called Calvin.

"Hey. Are you good?"

"Yes. I'm thinking of changing my name," he said.

"I'm not surprised, Zion. Hmmmmm. I think I can get used to that."

Chapter 23

(Reasons)

Once she finished checking on The Kitchen, Gabby headed directly to Santana County Hospital. I had updated her on Greta's condition and was there waiting for her.

It was such a relief to see her when she arrived. I so desperately needed the huge hug she gave me. I almost melted from both fatigue and emotional distress.

"I am so happy to see you, G," I confessed as we both sat.

"I'm sorry I wasn't here. Is there anything new?" she asked.

"Yes." I happily and with even more relief said, "She is stable. She had a good night. If she continues to do well, they will move her out this afternoon or this evening."

"Thank God!" Gabby said expressing heartfelt gratitude.

"Yes! Thank God. And I talked to her this morning for a minute or two."

"What did she say?"

"Girl! YOU know!" I was almost too angry to tell her. "She worried about Cameron! She asked me to take care of him!"

"Jesus! She loves that man! Good thing he loves her too!"

I choose not to respond to her statement.

Gabby continued to ask, "So what happened? What is really going on?"

"She sat at the bar; I was making her breakfast. We were talking and suddenly, she just passed out. It was crazy!" I explained.

"Oh, my Goodness!!!"

"Yes. She was completely unconscious, but she was breathing and had a pulse. I called 9-1-1 and then checked her blood pressure which was sky high. But mostly I just prayed and talked to her."

"Wow. I'm glad she was with you when it happened and not alone."

Gabby saying that, was the first time that I realised that had she been alone and had I not taken off for Kevin, she certainly could have died.

"I'm glad she was there," I said. "It was crazy."

"But why was she there for breakfast?"

"Oh. She had spent a night or two with me…" I awkwardly said.

I did not want to say much.

"Why? What are you trying not to tell me? And why?"

Gabby was beginning to feel left out.

I knew I needed to tell her something.

"She and Cameron had a fight, and she came over and stayed with me. Which was just a blessing because he would have already been at work when she passed out."

I explained, hoping she would pick up on the blessing as opposed to getting to the bottom of the reason for the fight between the two of them.

"Wow. But, God!" she said.

"Amen. If I'm being completely honest, I had not thought about it this way. I was upset with Cameron about whatever their argument was that caused her to get upset. But I guess that's the thing about God, He can see so far beyond us and even when things seem to be sent to break us or hurt us or even destroy us – he makes it for our good. She likely would have died had she not been there with me. Wow!"

I felt a sense of shame, but at the same time happy to have treated him fairly. I am just reminded again that God is in control.

"But you were in New Orleans with Calvin?" I asked.

"Ah, G! You cannot believe what happened" she was shaking her head as though she did not believe either.

"What?"

I was intrigued.

"Well, I told you he's from New Orleans. He got a call from his friend there saying his stepmother was dying and asking for him. When he told me about it, I asked if I could fly down with him. Girl, tell me how, he got the information, flew down there, saw her and talked to her, got a box of his very own history lesson and saw the woman dead and cremated in less than thirty-six hours?"

"Whoa! What?"

She took me too fast. I know I missed a lot of that!

"G," she said, "the man's name was never supposed to be 'Calvin' – his name was supposed to be 'Zion Alexander Baptiste'!"

"Wait," I said, "you are really taking me too fast! How?"

"Well, they had already named him and called him Zion for months before he was born. And when his mum died in childbirth, his father lost it. Blamed Calvin, changed his name to some name he saw on a hospital worker!"

Gabby was shaking her head.

I was blown away. "Wow!"

"So, when we got there his step mum, Carla – is sickly and feeble and she has this oxygen tank, God rest her soul – she confessed that she took a DVD his father had recorded for him, because she was jealous of his father's feelings for his dead mother! And girl! That DVD!"

She took a deep, deep breath.

"I wish you could see it!" Gabby was still amazed.

I was all in. This is so bizarre. Who does that?

"So how is Calvin handling all of this?"

I was curious.

"He seems to be handling it surprisingly well. I am amazed at the way he could discern this and discern that, then pull out whatever he needed to make himself stronger. Amazing man! He said he is thinking of taking his original name though. Zion."

"Really? Changing his name?" I asked. "That's huge!"

"Calvin says he never felt like *Calvin* and wondered what his life would have been as Zion. And you know, he seemed like a different person from the time his father said his full name at the end of the DVD and told him that he loved him. It was powerful!"

"Wow," I said. "I cannot imagine what all of that must feel like to him. So, what was it like being there with him?"

She smiled broadly.

"Amazing in more ways than I can possibly tell you."

"That's a good thing," I said.

"How is Kevin?" she asked.

"Oh, he's fine. He went in to work today. I need to go by the firehouse and see him. I need to go to the office and work on the schedule. But I also need to be here. I promised, Cam."

"I'm here now." She offered. "Go do some things. Whatever you need to do. I will call you if things change here. I got at least a couple of hours."

I really needed that, so I took her up on the offer.

(Soul Deep in Love)

And my soul was just aching to see Kevin.

I called him before I left so when I arrived, he was standing outside the firehouse waiting for me. I got out of the car, I needed to be in his arms.

As I stood there in his arms, somehow, everything seemed right. He was like home, my go to place, my recharging station.

"Are you good baby?" he asked.

"I am now," I said.

He began to rock me, ever so slightly, ever so gently. I was so peaceful on the inside, swaying, fully loved. I did not want to let go.

He kissed me. Why does this man always taste so good? So fresh, so tasty, so inviting! Jesus! I think he does it on purpose.

"How is Greta?" he asked.

"She's stable. They may move her out of the ICU in a few hours."

"And Cameron?"

"He is doing good. It's tough. But he's doing good."

He was looking into my eyes and still swaying me in his hug while asking, "What are you about to do?"

"I need to run by the apartment first, then I'm going to the office, I need to work on the schedule. Only I don't want to stop doing this."

I smiled at him, and he kissed me again.

I pulled away from him to make the quick run home then go to the job.

As I rode home, I diverted from my usual gospel music. I just needed to hear a little bit of a love song. I like Major. I like *'This Is Why I Love You'*. I ended up playing it fully through three times before I got home. I sat and listened to the end of it before deciding to get out of the car.

All I could think of heading to my apartment was that I am *soul* deep in love with this man. He was all I believed that I would ever want in a man. I knew that I was really and truly, completely in love.

Suddenly I heard a horn blowing, and the person was laying on it! I looked up and the car was almost upon me!

"Dammit!"

I looked in the car as it passed me – are you ready for this? It was the crazy Michelle, smiling.

Chapter 24

We were a less than a week away from Christmas and all of our lives were in some way affected with negative vibes. You already know the tragedy with Greta. Oliver had already been making Gabby's life difficult, and surely when he finds out about how close she and Calvin really were, that would be a problem.

And me? I was dealing with madness with Kevin's ex-wife. I really didn't know if she was trying to hit me with her car or just scare me. One thing for certain, she wanted me to know that it was her. I did not tell Kevin. I did not know what to do about it really. Other than make sure I always keep my pepper spray handy. As a matter of fact, I needed to try it to be sure that it worked.

Once I completed the staff schedule, I decided to ask Jason – the world's most handsome security guard to walk me to my car. I didn't know, maybe she followed me here.

This woman had me paranoid – but it's still better safe than sorry.

Of course, I could never really come in here and not get caught up in an emergency. We have a two gunshot wounds coming in. I stopped by the desk, without going into the belly of the O.R., that way I would not have to change into scrubs.

"Hey? What we got?"

"Hey, Ms Giselle. I didn't know you were here."

Kiara was our unit secretary, noticeably young and energetic, though sometimes more interested in the physicians than her actual tasks – she brought a much-needed likableness to the unit.

"A fifteen-year-old and a seventeen-year-old, shot by a six-year-old. Found his dad's gun. They said he was playing. But still got two shots off before he realised what was going on." Kiara told me.

"Are you serious?"

I was shaking my head. Because I am not a gun advocate. I never have been. I believe they only serve to make situations worse the vast majority of the time.

"How bad are they?"

Seventeen-year-old is critical, already in Trauma 13. They started about five minutes ago. He has a gunshot wound to the abdomen. Fifteen-year-old was hit in the foot."

"Parents here?"

"Mum is. Dad not here yet."

Still shaking my head.

"I really hope he makes it."

The intercom from Trauma 13 lit up.

"We need four units packed cells and a six-pack of platelets." The O.R. nurse said.

I asked, "Has he been typed and screened, or do we just have to go for it?"

"We sent blood for a type and screen, but it's not possible that it's ready. Can you send somebody here to get the request slips? I already called the blood bank. I can't leave!"

"Of course," I said. "You get the slip," I said to the unit secretary, "I will go for the blood products."

And with that I was thrust in the middle of a full-blown unfortunate emergency. All the time I was running to the blood bank, I was praying for that kid. By the time I got there, the O.R. had requested three more units of packed red blood cells. He was bleeding out quicker than they could stop the bleeders.

"Jesus."

Suddenly I was running with a cooler full of blood products praying for this child's life and thinking how I hated guns.

I will not keep you in suspense. The kid required the immediate Mass Transfusion Protocol. Another 6 Plus 6 (6 units of Blood and 6 units of Plasma) was ordered as I was arrived in the OR. Then another. And Another. He made it to the ICU, but he will have a colostomy and an ileostomy for the rest of his life. If he lives, he will have a long recovery period and his family will never be the same.

Sometimes I really hate being a nurse. All the time, I hate guns.

I did not forget to have Jason from security to walk me to my car. But I was so drained and so sad for the family, that my issue with Michelle really paled in comparison.

(Stable)

Greta had been moved to a private room on the Surgical Ob-Gyn unit. Cameron was at her bedside, holding her hand while she slept, and Gabby was texting with Calvin. I popped my head in before going home because I needed to see her.

I did not want to wake her or disturb Cam. I did a quiet finger to lip 'Shhhh' and silently moved over to Gabby. We walked out into hallway.

"Hey, how long has she been out of ICU," I asked.

"About an hour."

She looked at me oddly.

"What's wrong?"

"Two kids, gunshot wounds," I said shaking my head.

"Dead? Drugs, gang related?" She assumed.

"No. Dad's gun, younger sibling. Don't worry. It will be all over the news if it's not already."

"Wait, it was already! I saw that on 11 p.m. news highlights a few minutes ago."

She remembered.

"Are they okay?"

"One of them, yes. The other one is still alive but critical," I said. "I'm going home."

"Me too," she said.

We opened the door and quietly waved to Cameron.

Gabby said, "I will see you at 7 in the morning, Cam. Try to rest."

We both then walked out together.

As we were walking, I thought about Michelle and decided to share.

I stopped walking and said, "G, guess what happened to me after I left here today?"

"I don't know. What?"

"Girl! Michelle ran upon me with her car, blasting her horn! She could have hit me!"

"Wait, are you serious?"

"Of course, I'm serious!" I exclaimed. "It was crazy!"

"Did you tell Kevin or call the police or anything?"

"No," I said, "I just went inside."

"Where were you?"

"At my apartment!"

"She's crazy," Gabby said. "You need to get a restraining order or something. She is crazy!"

"I know."

"What do you have for protection?" she asked quite concerned, maybe even more than I was.

"I have pepper spray," I said. "I have a taser too, but you know I try to keep it hidden."

"You better take that thing out and put it in a holster. Sooner or later, she is coming directly at you!"

"You think?"

"I do. And you better think it too. She's crazy, G. Be careful."

I already knew that, but I guess hearing her say that put me on notice like I was not before. I touched my pocket to feel for my pepper spray, which was there.

This is the reason I really don't like relationships. Just too much drama.

(Unstable)

I very carefully scanned my surroundings before getting out of my car when I arrived home. I looked for Michelle's car and it was not in the parking lot, so I knew I was safe, for tonight anyway.

I headed to my apartment still thinking about those young men and their family from tonight. For a moment I forgot there was a problem with a crazed female. And I really don't know how she did it. But no sooner than I took a few steps out of the car, she was there.

"Hi, bitch," she said with a smile on her face.

"What do you want?" I exhaustedly asked, even though I was totally shocked.

"I don't know," she said, "maybe to beat your ass. That might make me feel better."

"Well and it might not!" I warned her. "You know it won't get you back with Kevin, right? You do know that? Right?"

"I decided that I don't want him back. I just want to beat your ass," she explained.

Shaking my head and initially attempting to walk away from her.

"Pitiful," I said.

"You think you are so high and mighty. So much better than me?" she said while blocking my path.

"You think you are so much better than I am!" She very angrily repeated.

"Well, that's not true." I said.

I took a step back to not be so close to her.

"I don't think I'm better than anyone. As for you, I don't even *think* about you (I made sure to speak in a disdainful manner. I could tell that bothered her)."

"Not at all. Not ever." I added. "Unless it's to feel sorry for you. Because you are probably the most pathetic person I know. Do you even know *how* to go away?" I asked. "Why are you still hanging around where you are not wanted? Didn't Kevin tell you to go away?"

She looked at me, nodded and said, "You don't even think about me. Huh? I'm not worth a thought from you?"

"Girl, no, *Woman*! You are a grown ass woman! Please! I am not doing this with you. And *NO,* I don't think about you! Not in the least! I mean, for what?"

"Well maybe you should, bitch!"

With that, she slapped me so hard that I saw a flash of light and went temporarily blind in my left eye. I was not able to stand and hit the ground hard. It was unexpected, and it disoriented me. I tried to shake it off, but she started to kick me. I had to *think* of how to fight back, but this bitch felt like three bitches were beating my ass!

I managed to grab her foot as she kept stomping and kicking me, and I was able to make her fall, so we were on the ground fighting each other. Then this bitch started throwing fists! Who am I fighting? Mike Tyson? I scratched every part of her face I could touch, fortunately I had well-manicured strong nails!

She punched me in the face and her finger went into my mouth. I grabbed on to that finger with my teeth and held on for dear life. I tried to bite it off. I then remembered that I had pepper spray in my pocket. Thank God I was able to get it out. I tried to blind that hoe! But some pepper spray got on me too.

She began to try and fight the pepper spray instead of me and I heard a male voice yelling, "Stop it! Stop it!"

It was Sean from my building. He came and broke us up. He asked if I wanted to call the police.

I said, "Definitely!"

Before the police arrived, she had gotten into a different car and left.

I completed the police report, including all her previous antics and bullying. The officer suggested and I agreed to file a restraining order on tomorrow. But I didn't decide to tell Kevin. Maybe I was pushing in some way for this fight. I knew she was unstable. I'm not sure why I wasn't trying to defuse it. But I was sick of her bullying me. And I was not afraid.

But truth be told, after that, I don't want to fight anymore, ever. I left hoping we had both had enough of fighting each other. I left hoping she had enough and didn't want to fight or have any contact with me anymore as well.

Chapter 25

Cameron remained at Greta's bedside. He held her hand and as much as he could and tended to her every need. He worked to keep her comfortable – adjusting the bed, the pillows, bringing and removing blankets. He helped her up to the bathroom, as well as walked beside her in the hallway post-surgery.

But he knew that was not enough.

Greta was fully awake.

He sat holding her hand.

"I want to tell you something," he said.

Greta looked at him. Then dropped her eyes from his.

"No, babe," Cameron said immediately, "look at me. Please."

She looked directly into his eyes but did not say a word. She waited for him to speak.

He sighed heavily, then spoke the most honest words he had ever said in his life.

"I'm sorry. And I know you don't want to hear that right now. But I'm so sorry. Can you ever forgive me?"

"What are you asking me to forgive you for?" Greta asked quietly. "I need you to say it. Because to be honest, I don't know what you are asking me for? I don't know what you want."

"Everything that I said the night you left, was wrong. I was wrong. I was selfish and I was only thinking about myself. It is finally obvious to me, that I gave not one single thought to what you were going through and what you needed. I was only thinking about what I wanted and what I felt."

A single tear fell down his face, and he wiped it with a quickness and held his head in a stronger state.

"I understand what I've done," he said. "But I promise you I can be a much better man that that. If you can let me."

She looked away and tears flowed down her face.

He quickly got facial tissues to wipe her tears then returned to holding her hand.

She continued to look away from him, shaking her head.

"I don't know where we are anymore. I just don't know", she said.

"That's fair. I really don't know if I deserve another chance." He admitted.

"Right, because you are an imperfect man. I know. Your favourite excuse" she sarcastically reminded him.

"Baby, no. I'm done with excuses, and you are right that sounds like me. But that was the old me. And I was wrong. I know that. I was selfish and I was no doubt, a strong reason for where we are right now." He further admitted.

"But maybe, Greta, maybe you can come back, and I can help you heal in the comfort of your own home, while you decide" Cam suggested.

She looked toward him briefly, then again turned away in the complete opposite direction from him.

"I won't be discharged tomorrow and maybe not the next day. But I don't know what I'm going to do right now. I just don't know. And I can't think about it."

Cam nodded his head.

"Okay, okay. I'm sorry."

She began to grimace and hold her incision site on her lower abdomen.

"Greta, do you need pain medicine? Let me give you pain medicine."

He pressed the IV pump and delivered the medication.

"Are you comfortable? Too hot, too cold? Do you need anything?"

Cam was at her beck and call.

"No, I just want to rest."

Soon thereafter she drifted off to sleep.

Cameron stayed watch over her.

(Oliver's Awakening)

The kitchen had already closed for the night and Oliver was putting the finishing touches on before closing. Gabby walked in and had a seat at one of the tables. She waited for him to finish.

Oliver headed out, keys in hand and was surprised to see her sitting there.

"Hey," he said somewhat puzzled. "I didn't expect to see you tonight. I didn't hear you come in."

"Do you have time to sit with me, to talk with and listen to me?"

She quietly requested.

He put his keys back in his pocket and said, "Yeah, sure," then sat with her.

"Oliver, there is so much about you that is amazing. And you did an incredible thing for me. I don't know how I would have made it, without you at that time. I really don't. That's why I'm talking to you now."

"Am I fired?"

He expected so.

"Not yet."

She answered.

"And I don't want to fire you. But I will. What are you doing? Why do you keep doing these things concerning Calvin and my personal life? Why are you relentless on this?"

"I don't want you to want him. Anyone else, no problem. Just not him. Not him, Gabby." He was continuously shaking he head 'no' as he voiced his one thing.

"But it *is* him," she said, "It *is* him and only him."

"Why?" he asked almost angrily, defiant and agitated manner possible.

"Because I'm married?"

"You do remember that before you were even in the picture, he was the picture? You remember that right? I've always had this thing for him. I can't explain it."

"But he hurt you."

"He did, but I hurt him too, Oliver. You know that. I could have handled whatever happened between he and I much better. I put us in a bad place as much as he did. I wanted to hurt him if I'm being honest. So, I shut him off instead of talking to him the way a woman should."

Oliver gave a sarcastic laugh.

"Now you are blaming yourself, making excuses for him."

"Geeze, Oliver! I know you are better than this!"

"Better than wanting the best for you?"

"Oliver!" She quickly interjected. "You don't get to determine what is or is not best for me! You get it?"

The anger resonated in her voice, loudly.

They were both quiet for a few seconds.

Gabby broke the silence.

"Oliver, I want you to decide right here, right now. You decide. Either you stay out of my personal life or get up, walk out and never look back. I've had enough."

He could tell she meant it, but she had meant it before, and they kept finding themselves in the same place.

"I'm going to try," he said.

"Well. No." She informed him.

"You are going to do it – one or the other. Because we are not going through anything else. The next thing that happens, I am going to ask your fully committed, super white teeth, beautiful, petite wife to stop you. AND I am going to fire you. Do you understand?"

"Wow!"

He was caught off guard. He somewhat shook it off, stood to his feet and said, "I will see you tomorrow."

"I hope so," Gabby said, "Just under a completely different understanding."

He took his keys out of his pocket, looked at her for a couple of heartbeats then turned to leave.

"Oliver. You are important to me in more ways than one. I really hope you can stay."

He gave a slight nod.

"Goodnight."

He headed out.

"Goodnight," she said.

(I Love You – Whoever You Are)

Gabby could hardly wait to get home; Calvin was there, and she was just ready to see him again. When she arrived, he was asleep on the sofa, holding the picture of the family. The DVD player was on, but nothing was playing. The DVD had ended and was on the screen saver. She knew what had been happening.

She leant and kissed him on his forehead, and he woke immediately.

"Hi," he said.

"Hi. Are you good?"

He laughed.

"It depends on how you define good. I'm good physically, but I am thrown completely off balance emotionally."

"I can imagine," she said. "I think anyone would be. You been through a lot in a truly short period of time. I would be thrown for sure."

"You want to hear something funny?" he asked.

"I think I may have watched that DVD twenty times today, maybe more. I needed to see it over and over."

"That makes sense to me, Calvin," she said and sat next to him.

He placed his hand on her knee.

"Thanks. I can't believe you. You're here with me through all of this – or at all really. I'm trying to figure out who I am right now…"

She dropped her forehead on his and said, "That's okay. I love you, whoever you are."

She quickly stood.

"Now. What's for dinner?"

"You are!"

He gave a sly smile.

"I'm with that!"

She gave a coy look and smiled back.

Calvin stood and wrapped his arms around her waist.

"I really mean it when I say thank you. I am better with this whole thing because of you. I'm going back to work tomorrow. Try to get back to normal. Christmas is only three days away. Wow! What would be the perfect gift for you?" he asked pensively.

"Are you asking me for an answer, or do you think you know?"

"I know what I want to give you," he said. "By the way, what time are you going to The Kitchen tomorrow?"

"Well, I'm sitting with Greta until about nine or ten. I told Cameron I would come back and relieve him at 6."

"Call me tomorrow when you leave the hospital. And in the meantime, I am ready for dinner!"

He reminded her.

They laughed and both nodded.

Chapter 26

(Peace)

The following morning, Oliver opened The Kitchen and there were already hungry patrons coming in and out. But none surprised him more than when Calvin walked in the door.

The two men looked at each other. It almost seemed that no one else was in the room. Calvin broke the silence.

"Morning."

A bit hesitant, Oliver, going through his mind of why Calvin was there blurted, "Look, Gabby, is not here. She will be late today. She's at the hospital."

"I know," Calvin said. "I came to talk to you. Is that possible?"

Oliver could think of no legitimate reason why not.

"Sure. Have a seat."

The men sat across from each other. Calvin had walked in with an orange juice and sat it on the table after taking a sip from the straw. He took a deep breath.

"It's been a crazy thing between the two of us," Calvin said. "I want to talk it out. I want to squash it. I want us to have peace because that is what Gabby needs."

Oliver was not sure why Calvin was doing this. But he knew that it was the right thing to do. He offered an apprehensive 'Okay'.

"I really don't know where we got off on the wrong foot," Calvin said "but it seemed that from the first moment we met, you had something against me. Is there something I need to know?"

"No. Not at all," Oliver said quickly, "but I knew you would hurt her. And you did. I've seen men like you all my life. I've seen how they treat women."

Calvin momentarily closed his eyes and breathed deeply.

"I'm going to ask you, Oliver, to not judge me at all, but definitely not based on what you know or believe about somebody else. I think that's a good place to start. You see, man, you don't *know* me. You don't *know* my life. You don't *know anything* about me. Just that you don't like me. What good comes from that?"

Oliver looked him in the eyes as though he expected a flinch or glance away. Not the case.

"So, you are real about this. Why? What is your real angle, man? What do you get out of making *peace* with me?" Oliver was suspicious but interested to hear the reason.

Calvin needed to make one thing clear and boldly let it out saying, "I'm NOT afraid of you, man. Not in the least. Don't put yourself up too high in this false sense of superiority!"

He quickly paused, remembering why he came.

He again took a deep breath and said, "It's not for me. I'm not doing this for me. It's not about what I get out of it. It's for Gabby. She respects you as her chef, she appreciates you as a friend. She loves me and I love her. She wants you here and I know she needs you here. But I know that our feuding is taking a toll on her AND on me. It's not good. So, I'm no longer participating."

"You're no longer participating?" He scoffs first then thinks about it.

"No, I'm not." Calvin added in complete candour, "But I can promise you that I also am not leaving."

"Okay. I understand. You know what? You are right. She will pick you. You remind me of someone my mum dated. Almost identical in look and behaviour. When he didn't want her anymore, he just left. Up and left. What happens when you don't want Gabby anymore? Just leave her and then I'm there trying to pick up the pieces. Well, you know what, Calvin (getting louder), sometimes the pieces can't be picked up and people turn to drugs and alcohol. And you know what? Sometimes they die!"

"Is that what happened to your mum?"

"Fuck you, man!" Oliver shouts full of anger, clearly affected on a deeper and personal level than their conversation should prompt.

"No! Is that what happened to your mum?"

Calvin shouts back, not letting it go.

"Yes! As a matter of fact, it was *exactly* what happened! Now what?" Oliver demanded.

Calvin returns to a calm voice.

"That wasn't me, man. That's not me."

"Right."

Oliver was in the throes of misplaced anger.

"Look I don't have to prove anything to you. Not anything at all, Oliver (He paused)." "But I don't just *want* her, I love her, and I need her. And she loves me too."

Calvin paused for a moment then added, "I personally think we can all coexist. We just have to decide to."

Oliver was quiet. Both men looked in opposite directions of each other. Thinking.

Again, Calvin broke the silence.

"I'm sorry about your mother, man. She didn't deserve that, and you didn't deserve to live through it or with it."

Oliver ran his fingers through his hair, removing his hairnet in the process.

"This is crazy." Oliver said to himself.

"Why?"

"I don't know," Oliver said, and he really didn't know why it was crazy, but it was.

Why had he just shared something so personal with this man, this man he hated. Had he been wrong about him all the time?

Quiet overtook the conversation. Calvin looked at his phone and Oliver did as well.

Calvin again took the lead, placing his phone on the table and looking at Oliver.

"Peace, man," he said and extended his hand to Oliver to shake.

Oliver initially hesitated but quickly came around and extended his own hand, shaking Calvin's and said, "Peace."

Both men sat back against their seat and breathed a sigh of relief.

Oliver laughed as he looked at Calvin.

"You really do remind me of that son of a…" he caught himself and did not finish.

"Well, I won't call him what I want to call him. But you look almost identical to him!"

He shook his head and laughed more.

"Yeah, man," Calvin said rather quickly. "But I'm not him. You cannot judge me by somebody in your past regardless of whether I look like them or not. Dammit!"

"Maybe I was wrong man. Apologies," Oliver said.

"It's done. It's over. No apology necessary. Just respect moving forward. I will do the same thing."

Calvin stood, then Oliver.

He and Oliver slapped hands into a strong shake, then said goodbyes.

Calvin looked around The Kitchen as they were leaving. He stopped and asked "Hey, man, what are you doing say around midnight tonight?"

Perplexed Oliver stopped before he got to the door and turned to Calvin.

"Just with my family and sleeping. Why?"

"Well, if you are game, I have an idea" Calvin said.

(The Whole Story)

Gabby relieved Cameron at 6 a.m. and had time to talk with Greta. She did not know what really happened concerning he and Greta. She knew there was an argument, and that Greta stayed the night away, but she did not know the depths of pain he had created until now. She was so horrified, as Greta told her the whole story, that she found tears and excessive anger creeping upon her.

"And I just don't see how I can go back to him," Greta said.

Greta wasn't crying and maybe not even sad about it anymore. "I don't know that I can see him in my future or that I even want to."

"Wow. I understand, Greta. I would probably feel the same way."

"It's really hard to imagine that he did that, said those things." Gabby said shaking her head.

"I knew he was going through a lot. I knew he was trying to handle it, but to believe such things about me and the way he said it – so angry, so cold and hateful, blaming me – I can never forget that," Greta said.

"So, what is he doing now? Does he know what you are thinking right now?" Gabby asked. "I mean, he is probably the most supportive, dedicated and loving man I've ever seen during this."

"I think there are two Camerons. One – is the most amazing man I've ever met or could ever hope to meet, but the other Cameron – I could not be sorrier that I ever met him." Greta confessed.

"And no, I haven't told him that I've decided not to go home with him when I am discharged. I just know that I can't do it. That I know with great certainty."

She gives a slight bit of thought to the possibility of returning home then reinforces her statement.

"No. I cannot. I don't want to. There's too much," she said. "I'm going to tell him when he gets back. He asked about it. He has apologised. But I'm done here."

"I'm sorry to hear that. I always loved the two of you together. It felt a bit like hope for me," Gabby said.

"Yes, I know," Greta said reminiscing. "And maybe at some point he was that for me too. But I don't feel it anymore."

Greta paused for a moment then asked, "But you are in love, right? You have found something great with Calvin. Right?"

"Yes. Maybe like never ever before."

Gabby reflected.

"With Travis, we were together since we were kids. There was no real comparison. Not to denigrate what we had in the least; it was beyond amazing. But this is adult, real-life stuff that shakes you to your core. Calvin gives me emotions I have never had and love I have always wanted. In essence, he gives me love I never ever expected to find after Travis died. And to be honest, I really didn't even know to want it."

"Great." Greta was bit lacklustre but added, "You deserve that. We all deserve that kind of love."

"I know things are really messed up right now, Greta, but it won't last," Gabby said. "Because things have a way of getting better when you least expect them to. But mainly because God's got you. He loves you. He knows how much you love Him. And ALL things work together for the good of those who love Him and are called according to His purpose. Trust that He knows exactly what He is doing. I know that's easier said than done. But guess what? God knows it too. He's got you; He's got us."

Cameron arrived with a huge bouquet of pink roses.

Gabby reacted before Greta could a word.

"Whoa! How many roses is that?" She gasped.

Cameron laughed.

"Only three dozen, come on!"

He placed the roses on the windowsill and leant over to kiss Greta. She did not move. He kissed her on the cheek.

Gabby stood.

"I will see you later, sis. Call me if you need me! Cam, really nice roses!"

She smiled at them both then left the room.

Chapter 27

(Discharged)

Cameron sat next to Greta and held out his hand to her. She reluctantly held his hand but found it difficult to look at him.

He could feel it, the great loss he had caused.

"I'm sorry, baby."

He took her hand in both of his.

"I'm really sorry. I wish I could go back and undo everything. I would do everything differently. I really do wish I could change this."

Greta could not cry. In an odd way, she wanted to. But over the past four or five days she had dried every tear duct that she had.

"Me too, Cameron."

She looked at him, removed her hand from his and interlocked her own fingers then lay them across her tummy. "But neither of us can go back," she said solemnly.

Dr Jordan arrived, knocked on the door first then entered before the okay to enter came.

"Good morning."

They both greeted her then waited for her to speak.

"How do you feel, Greta?" she asked as she touched Greta's abdomen and looked at her incision site.

"I'm okay," she said. "I had a bowel movement, I'm up and walking. I don't need shots for pain anymore. I'm okay."

"Do you think you are ready to go home?"

"I think I'm probably ready to be discharged. I can heal just as well out of the hospital as in, I guess."

"Okay," Dr Jordan said. "Tomorrow is Christmas Eve, thought you might like to be with family, if you met the markers and you have so far. But I want you to see me in a week. And I also want you to talk to somebody. You have been through a lot. I want to have my office make an appointment with a postpartum specialist that we use. Okay?"

Hmmmmm, Greta thought.

"Do I really need that?"

"Yes, Greta, you really need that. And it may also be a good idea for you to join her Cameron. You both have had traumatic experiences. I'm serious this time. I want you to promise me. I want you to commit to six sessions. If you do not believe it is helping, stop them. But commit to the six, okay?"

She dropped a parental type of look.

"Promise me, Greta."

Deep sigh.

"Okay, I promise. *SIX* sessions – that is all I am committing to though!"

"That's good enough."

Dr Jordan looked at Cameron.

"She will be discharged at 8 in the morning. I need to set everything up today. I'm going to leave her prescriptions at the desk today. You can fill them today if you would like to."

Cameron nodded.

Dr Jordan left without knowing that she had created a need for Greta to face Cameron and tell him her decision. She began to sit up on the bedside and Cameron rushed to help her. She immediately raised her hand to halt his movement

"No. I got it."

"Let me help you, Greta."

He needed to help her, maybe for himself, maybe to make sure she was okay. But he needed to help her.

She looked at him and shook her head.

"No. I need to do this myself. I only want to sit up in the chair by myself."

"Okay, baby."

"And we need to talk."

Greta added.

Cameron watched her carefully as she sat in the chair. Then straightened the covers on her bed.

"Do you need a blanket?"

"No. I just want to sit here for a while."

She then reached to the windowsill where her robe was draped, took it and spread it from her waist to her feet.

Cameron sat on the bed. He dropped his head, then looked up at her. She was already looking at him.

"I cannot go home with you tomorrow," she said.

"I guess I was expecting that."

He shrugged his shoulders.

"I can't. Not yet. If ever," she admitted.

"I know," he said. "I know what I did. I don't know how to fix it. But I know it needs to be fixed."

He dropped his head in his hands again, then looked up and asked, "Do you know where you are going? What are you going to do? Do you want me to leave? That's really the best thing, I guess. I should leave."

"Cam, I don't ever want to go back there. Not ever. Not *ever* again."

Cameron started.

"I will find a place where you…"

She cut him off.

"I don't want you to find a place. I want you to just let me figure this out! Please!"

Quiet overtook the room.

"Should I leave now?" Cameron asked.

"Maybe," she said.

But she could not look at him.

"I will be at the restaurant. Will you call me?" he asked hoping for a yes.

She finally looked at him.

"For what?"

"Maybe I can take you wherever you want to go when you are discharged. I can pack a bag for you. I know you need to be away from me, but at least let me help you safely get to where you need to be. And I know I don't deserve that opportunity."

"You know what?"

She conceded.

"Yes, you can do all of that. But only if you arrive here tomorrow with an attitude of moving forward. Not poor pitiful you *or* me! This thing is horrible, but we cannot let it swallow us. If you can come strong and ready, fine. Otherwise, I will ask you to leave as soon as you get here. I want you to rest tonight. If you want to call me tonight, okay. But call me with hope not sadness. You must take care of yourself because I cannot take care of both of us. And yes, I would appreciate if you would pack a bag for me. A big bag, maybe two."

"Okay," he said. "Thanks."

He headed dejectedly to the door.

"Funny," Greta said just as he began to reach for the door, "I just realised that tomorrow is Christmas Eve, when Dr Jordan said it."

"I knew," he said. "I was hoping we would be together for Christmas. That's all I've been hoping for – you to be out and much better by Christmas. Looks like God has answered that prayer anyway."

"Yeah. I guess so."

She agreed.

"Try to find your strength, Cam. I know it's in there."

He nodded and left the room.

He immediately came back inside before allowing the door to close completely and said to her, "I need you to know one thing."

"What is that?' she asked.

"I am not going to let *us* be lost because of this. I'm not, Greta. We will overcome this, and we will be stronger than ever before," he said. "That's my promise to you."

"I will see you in the morning," she said.

She knew she did not see that promise coming to fruition.

Cameron left, this time, to return tomorrow to collect her.

(Still Roommates)

I decided to take Christmas Eve and Christmas Day off. After all, I was always on call, so it didn't matter. Since our schedule was light thanks to the holidays, the new schedule was complete, and I had been in the fight of my life, I was not going in the next two days. I leant back in my home office chair but felt the pain of the beating I had endured at the hands of a crazy woman. I knew that staying home to heal a bit, was the right decision.

I went to the bathroom and looked at my face again. The left side of my face was swollen from that power slap that I so graciously received; I just prayed that I didn't get a black eye. Her punches and kicks/stomps were hard but most of them were body shots, so while I was sore all over, she looked as though she got the worst end of the beatdown because of the scratches and pepper spray. She *looked* that way. But I was not claiming victory. I knew I wasn't likely to win, but all you must do is stand up to a bully. Show them you are not afraid to fight. Hopefully, you will not have to, but if you do, give it all you got.

As I looked at my wounds the phone rang. Greta.

"Hey, G," I said a bit surprised to hear from her.

"Hey," she said sounding stronger than I expected.

"I'm being discharged tomorrow. I was hoping I could crash at your place for a little longer."

"Of course," I said, "do you need me to pick you up?"

"No. Cam is going to do that. I will see you around ten or so. Is that good?" She needed confirmation. She didn't know how much time or help she would require.

"Of course. Are you sure you don't need me to pick you up?"

"Yes. Cameron is going to do that. He is also going to pack some things for me (She paused a bit then*). I told him that I can't come back home yet."*

"Are you okay?"

"I really am," she said, *"but not if I was going back there."*

"I understand" (and I really did).

"Just let me know if there's anything you need. Okay?"

"Sure. Thanks, G. See you tomorrow." She hung up.

(My Face)

The more I looked at that power slap mark, the more I could see her fingers on my face. Really! There are like ridges or something. I wondered what she was thinking. I wondered if her eyes were still burning. I wondered how that finger was feeling! I knew my kidney was still hurting. I was surprised that I was not pissing blood. I found the Epsom Salt and soaked for a long time.

I don't want to fight anymore. Ever.

I hadn't told Kevin about the fight, and he hadn't called and said anything about it, so I was fairly sure Michelle hadn't told him yet either. He would be back home tomorrow and Christmas day. I hoped he didn't think the fight was over him because it was not. Apparently, it was something that we needed to do.

And I had to file that order of protection. I didn't know where she lived, I just knew her name, assuming her last name was still Harper.

Wow. What a mess!

OMG! I hoped nobody made a video!

Chapter 28

Cameron arrived before 7 a.m. in preparation for Greta's discharge. He indeed picked up her medications the day before and had her bags packed and in the car. He knew the specific drinks she liked as well as her stress snacks. He purchased them all. He also bought fresh purple roses – distinctive to his regard to her as royalty in his life – his queen. But also, fresh pink roses which he knew were her favourite. But she would find this when she got to the car.

For now, it was simple 'good morning' and a sweet cup of Joe the way she liked it.

"Good morning," she said and accepted the coffee.

Greta was already dressed and ready to go, just waiting for the word from Dr Jordan. But there was an extreme sadness in her. Cameron felt it too.

"I'm only going to say this once," Cameron said. "And yes, you may kick me out of this room. But I'm so sorry, baby. I was so wrong. I could not have been more wrong."

He squatted on his knees in front of her as she sat in the chair.

"I beg you, yes, I *beg* you to forgive me."

Greta looked him with swollen eyes from an all-nighter of attempts at washing away the pain and agony of what was her life right now. She looked at him and said the only thing she could say.

"I don't know what you want me to say. You know that I cannot promise you anything right now."

"I want to ask you something," Cameron said.

"Go ahead."

"Greta, do you love me? Do you still love me?"

She looked at him and he patiently waited. He wanted her to think about it, even if it was to his detriment.

Greta finally took a sip of the coffee he had brought her. The sweet taste of coffee and caramel reminded her of happier days.

"The truth is Cameron," she answered as best and as truthfully as she could, "I just don't know. My feelings are so muddy right now. I can't even differentiate the actual pain from the emotional pain. Do you understand?"

"I do," he said, "and I am going to make this up to you. I know you can't see it right now. But I know *us.* And we are stronger than even this."

He put both hands on her knees.

"I promise, baby, I'm going to fix this," he whispered.

(Christmas Eve)

When Gabby arrived at The Kitchen, she noticed something strange. There were amazing holiday decorations that were not there the day before. The windows were festive, and she saw what proved to be a beautiful eight-foot blue spruce fully decorated in only red poinsettias and white dove ornaments. There was a huge red flowing bow from the top of the tree that dripped three long red ribbons spread equally apart, to the floor. The other decorations continued the theme of red and white poinsettias and doves. She was almost floored. She opened the door and saw Oliver. She laughed!

"What is this?"

She was smiling so broadly she could not contain herself. The tables were all decorated with the same theme and there were representations of the holiday from all cultures that celebrate during this time. She walked about looking at the beautiful dining room and the tree.

She looked at Oliver and asked, "You?"

"US," he said.

Then pointed behind her.

When she turned Calvin was standing there.

"Yes," Calvin said. *"US!"*

Befuddled Gabby visibly shook her head for clarity.

"Wait. WHAT! WHEN? HOW?"

She looked back and forth between the two men and they both laughed.

Calvin walked to her and put his arms around her waist.

"You like?"

"I love!"

She was still surprised.

"When?"

"Last night," Calvin said as he released the hug. "We talked yesterday and decided to give you something special for the holiday."

"Well, this is really a great gift, and I didn't see it coming!"

She admitted.

"Oh," Oliver said, "this is not your gift!"

"NO?" she asked.

"What is it then?"

The two men stood side by side, Calvin dropped his arm over Oliver's shoulder.

And Oliver said, "Peace."

"Peace." Calvin reinforced.

Gabby nearly cried.

"Peace between you two? Real *PEACE*?"

The two men said, "YES!!!" at precisely the same time, smiling.

"I wish I could take credit for it." Oliver added, "But it was all Calvin's idea. Not mine."

"Baby," she said looking at him and walked over.

They hugged and kissed, then she gave Oliver a big hug.

"This means everything to me," she said. "I don't want to call it a Christmas Miracle, but it might be close!"

They all laughed.

"Are you here to serve breakfast bags this morning?" she asked Calvin.

"I can do that," he said.

Breakfast bags had been prepared and the doors opened at 8 a.m. There would be carry out breakfast until 10 a.m, then carryout lunch until 2 p.m. and closed until the four-hour serving period on Christmas Day.

(My Eye)

Man! This morning, Christmas Eve, my left eye was red. Face a little swollen, but fewer finger marks. I was waiting for Greta to get here, and I still looked like I was in a fight! Kevin would be here in a few minutes, and I still needed to go file the order of protection against Michelle. Geeze!

When the doorbell rang, I knew it was him. I didn't know what I was going to say. I peeked out and indeed it was him. I opened the door and headed away quickly so he would not see my face yet.

"Good morning, baby!" I said very cheerfully as I walked away. I went to the fridge, and he came behind me and put his arms around my waist. He squeezed me so hard from the back and hit my *kicked spot!*

"OUCH!"

I yelled and pulled away from him!

"What???"

He jumped back and looked at me and saw my eye!

"What the hell?"

He stepped back.

"What happened to you?"

"I don't want to tell you," I said quietly and attempted to walk away.

"Babe!" he grabbed me by the arm and demanded.

"Tell me what happened?"

"Michelle beat my ass yesterday." I admitted.

"WHAT?"

He stepped completely away from me. He appeared angrier than I had ever seen him.

"Are you serious?"

"Yes I am. But I beat her ass too," I said, "she did not have an easy time. She knows she was in a fight."

He began to dial a number.

"NO!!!" I yelled at him.

"DO NOT CALL HER!!! This is not about you. I got this!!! Did she tell you we were in a fight? (He shook his head 'no')?"

"And I didn't tell you last night either, baby. Let us handle it."

"I am so upset right now. I need to talk to her." He was so adamant, and I could see the boil in him. "She never should have touched you," he declared.

But his interference will only make this situation far worse.

"Look, well first, Greta, is going to stay with me for some time, I have no idea how long. Second after she gets here and gets settled in, you are going to take me to file an order of protection against Michelle. I did a police report last night."

"What happened?" He asked still fuming.

"She was here waiting for me, baby. She said some things, I said some things, she said some things, I said some things. She didn't like what I said – so she slapped me, and it was on. Sean came by and broke it up. The police came and I filed a report. I told them about the other times she has come here and harassed me. He told me what to do."

"Are you pressing charges against her? You know you can press charges against her."

He was livid and seemed to want me to do more than a restraining order.

"Kevin." I assured him. "She does not want any more of me. I'm doing this for the sake of safety. But my gut instinct, she had enough of me last night."

"DAMMIT!" he said. "I can't believe this." He slammed his fist on the counter.

"Kevin, I need you to promise me that you are not going to say anything to her about this."
He looked in the opposite direction.
"Kevin," I said. "Look at me (He looked at me)."
"Please don't say anything."
I begged him.
Quiet and a deep sigh from him.
"Okay, baby."
He agreed then let out an even bigger sigh.
He commenced to hold me again. I pulled away.
"Aye!!!"
That kick spot and the punch spots! Need more Epsom Salts.

Chapter 29

(Separation)

When Greta and Cameron arrived, I had already prepared her room. They went inside and Cameron set up her things for her.

"Is there anything that you need right now?" he asked knowing it was time for him to go.

She shook her head.

"No."

"Well," he said, "I guess I will go then."

He hoped she would say, 'No, wait.' But she did not.

I knocked on the door before he left and said, "Hey, Kevin and I are going to go do this thing. We will be back maybe in a couple of hours. Are you going to be here, Cam?"

He looked back at Greta.

"Well, I want to be. At least until you can get settled in. Is that okay?" he asked her.

I'm not sure what the look was that she gave me, but she then looked to him and said, "Yes, of course. Thanks."

I could see Greta's struggle. But she could not see my kick spot, my punch pain and because I had not gotten close enough to her, so she could see my red eye, she did not know about the fight. I needed to do this, then I would return home and Cameron could leave.

"Do you want me to bring you anything back?" I asked attempting to ease the tension.

"No," she said.

Kevin and I left them there. Fact is they probably needed each other. They both were hurting.

(I Will Take Care of You)

Greta rested in bed, while Cam turned the TV on and sat quietly.

When she suddenly made a noise, he quickly looked at her, went to her side and asked, "Do you need to take something for pain?"

She was in pain.

"Yes."

He went directly to get water then brought the medicine, opening the pill bottle and putting the pill in her hand. He waited for the square bottle of water once she finished and place it on the nightstand near her.

"Thanks, Cam," she said.

"Baby, anything," he said then returned to his seat and soon Greta drifted off to sleep.

Again, she dreamed of Bridget. They were again in Africa watching the sunset. Greta was dressed in flowing yellow sundress with straps that fell off her shoulders just slightly. Bridget was dressed in a white blazer with a white tank and matching short pants. And in the dream, they began to have another conversation.

"Why do you keep coming to me, Bridget? What does this mean?" Greta asked.

"I'm here because you want me here."

"I don't know that I want you here, Bridge. I don't know what I want or what I need."

"I know you don't," Bridget said. "But you don't have to know right now. All you need to know is that everything is going to be alright."

"Bridget, everything is definitely *not* alright, and it cannot be!" Greta shouted.

"Yes. It is. It is the way it is supposed to be. It was always going to be this way. And everything with Cameron will be okay too."

"How do you know that?"

Greta was annoyed in her dream state.

"Just say I have it on good authority." Bridget rose. "I must go now. I don't think I will see you for a while."

"Why?" Greta asked standing with her.

"Because you don't need me, anymore," Bridget said.

"But what if I do?" Greta asked.

"What is happening to your dress?" Bridget pointed to her clothing.

Greta looked down and her dress was turning white.

Bridget's voice was in the air though she was gone when Greta looked up.

"Your fear is going to disappear. You already have a protector by your side. He will take care of you." Bridget's voice in the wind said.

Greta woke and Cameron was sitting on the bedside near her.

"You were having a nightmare," he said.

"It was Bridget. I've dreamed of her for days now. This time she left me. She had I had a protector by my side."

"I'm always here. I'm always going to be by your side. I will take care of you, if you let me," Cameron said. "I love you."

"We have to figure it out. I just need time."

"And I will give you all of the time you need as long as you let me." He promised.

"Is it okay for me to just hold you while you sleep? Maybe it will help you rest better."

"Okay," she said.

And he did.

And she rested.

(Plans)

I had filed the restraining order. I was not sure when she would be served, but Kevin supplied her address and that should make it easier. I initially started having second thoughts about filing. The fight was so bad for both of us, I felt relatively sure that she would leave me alone. Plus, she said she did not want Kevin anymore, just to beat my ass and she surely did that. But because she had stalked me for months now, I felt I had no choice. Well, she was not in the parking lot when we returned, not that I could see anyway. And we made it into the building without any surprises.

When we got inside my apartment, Cameron and Greta were snuggled together in bed and both asleep. So, we didn't bother them at all.

Kevin and I proceeded to one of the best parts of us, cooking together. This would be our first-time cooking Christmas dinner as a couple, and I was so excited. I was wearing this great lightweight turtleneck, so I did not have to worry about my vulnerable neck. And I had been eating Advil like M&Ms, so I felt a bit better from the beatdown. I just had to watch my kick/stomp spots a little and keep eye away from the heat. And I could do that.

Then I had this great idea.

"Hey, babe," I said, "how about, since Greta and Cameron are here, what if I call and see if Gabby and Calvin are available for Christmas dinner here? This is the first time we have all had the opportunity to really celebrate like this. How would you feel about entertaining?"

"I think it's good," he said, "whatever you think, babe. Just make sure so we can cook enough and not too much."

I sat at the bar and called Gabby.

"Hi, G," I said, "I was wondering, if you and Calvin don't already have any special plans for Christmas dinner, maybe you guys could come over. Greta and Cameron are here, and Kevin and I would love if you could."

She was surprised at my saying Cameron was here.

"Wow, I didn't expect Cameron and Greta to be together after she was released," she said.

"I know." I agreed. "But there you have it."

"Let me ask Calvin. Hold on."

She returned after a few minutes asking, *"What time?"*

"4:30."

"Okay. We will be there."

"And please be on time, Gabby!" I asked reminding her, "It's Christmas, let's do it right, okay?"

"*Okaaaaaaaay!*" she exclaimed.

I was smiling and nodding to Kevin.

"It's a go, babe!"

I washed my hands and poured us both a glass of wine, then pulled the vegetable ingredients out of the fridge for chopping. He was already washing down the counterspace while preparing for us to get started.

"Hey," he said picking up his wine, "let's toast."

"Okay," I said, "to what."

He walked over to me and kissed me, quite nicely I might add.

"To us, you and me. I am really glad that I found you."

He tapped my glass but not before I said, "Me too."

"Okay, baby," he said. "Let's do this!"

He was baking and I was cooking sides. We had decided to purchase the protein and it was a great idea. *Honey Baked* ham and turkey, we were exceedingly fortunate to call and find it available. So, we only had to wait for delivery later this afternoon. I make an awesome sage stuffing, garlic green beans and mac and cheese. He claims that he can create an incredible freshly made walnut cranberry sauce – we will see.

We cooked until late in the night. We finished everything but the mac and cheese because I like to make it fresh for the guests, not overnight.

Cameron stayed the night with Greta, we saw him a time or two as we were cooking, when he got something either for Greta or himself to drink. The last time he came out, we asked him to dinner just to be sure and he accepted. His acceptance was with a bit of hesitancy. I'm sure he wanted to check with Greta. And I'm sure he will. But both he and Greta mostly kept to themselves in the guest bedroom all night.

Once we finished, I headed for the Epsom Salt bath.

Chapter 30

(Merry Christmas!)

Today is Christmas Day! We celebrate the coming of Christ. We celebrate love. We celebrate life and giving, just as Christ gave His life for us. That is who we are. That is where our hearts live and grow. Supreme thanks.

Kevin and I slept late then served at The Kitchen until 2 p.m. and made it home just after 3 p.m. Because we cooked last night, we had extraordinarily little to do. But the first thing I did was checked on Greta. I lightly knocked on her door.

"Come in," she said.

"Hi, G. How are you?"

"I'm okay, maybe even better than I thought I would be right now."

I looked around and no Cameron. The bathroom door was open, but I did not see or hear him.

So, I asked, "Where's Cam?"

"He went home to bathe. He told me about the dinner offer."

"I'm sorry. I know we should have asked you first." I admitted.

"No, I am glad you asked. I am happy that his Christmas will be here." She confessed. "I'm glad mine will be here too. Thank you, G."

"You never have to thank me." I said "I'm incredibly happy that you are here. You gave me the scare of my life you know!"

"I gave *me* the scare of my life!" she exclaimed laughing.

"Oh, Gabby and Calvin are coming over too. They are finishing up at The Kitchen and will be here in about an hour and a half."

She looked a little tired.

"I'm going to let you rest."

"No," she said shaking her head. "I want to tell you something."

"Okay," I said and sat on the bed near her as she lay there.

"I haven't changed my mind about Cameron" she confided. "I can't do it.

.

"Wow," I said, "I thought you two were working it out. I mean, he's here with you."

She nodded.

"I know. And he knows. I'm going to tell him again tonight. But I want us to have as good of a dinner as possible. He can stay tonight. But when he leaves to bathe and change, he will not come back. I'm going to tell him tonight; I don't know maybe in the morning. I need some time now."

"I understand," I said.

"What's up with your eye?" she asked looking at me strangely.

"I will tell you when Gabby gets here. I want to tell both of you together." I laughed. "It's really funny. You are going to get a kick (Oop!) out of it! Rest okay, I will let you know when dinner is ready."

"Nope," she said, "I will be out in a few minutes. Maybe I can help."

"Help what? Help who?" I asked.

"You can keep me company, but, sis, I need you to take care of yourself."

"I will" she assured me.

"Do you need me to help you get up, get dressed?"

"No. I want to do it myself. And Cam will be back. I'm letting him do everything he wants right now. I think he needs that."

"You still love him." I said, "How are you ever going to leave him? You're still trying to protect him, take care of him."

"Of course, I do. This is not at all about whether I love him or not. And I believe that he loves me too. But he doesn't treat me the way I need to be treated for our relationship to survive. It takes me to figure out if I can live with him as he is. I cannot hope for him to change. I have to know what I can handle."

I sighed loudly.

"You know, I get it, sis. I get it." I said.

I looked around the room and waited for her to say more. She did not. I put my hand on her foot and gave it a bit of a squeeze.

"I gotta go make some pasta for the mac and cheese. You know how you love my mac and cheese!"

She laughed and we heard the doorbell.

"Probably Cameron, huh?"

"Probably," she said.

Kevin had opened the door for him, and they briefly chatted, Cameron gave him two bottles of wine and offered thanks as well as to help prepare for the evening.

"No, man, we're good! Check on your girl."

"Hey, Giselle," Cameron said moving and looking toward the bedroom and seeing me.

"Hey, Cam," I said.

He was still somewhat of a shadow of the man he always was. I seem to feel worse for him by the moment. He went to his wife. About twenty minutes later they both emerged from the bedroom.

Greta jokingly said, "Forgive me, G, if I don't sit at the bar!"

And she took a seat on one of the steadier dining room chairs that Cameron had thoughtfully brought over.

"Uh, forgive me," I said, "if I don't let you sit at the bar!"

We both laughed. The guys didn't get it.

"Because she fell... never mind!"

I gave up the attempt to explain.

We turned on Christmas music, finished cooking and set the table. Suddenly I remembered. "We've never met Calvin!"

I looked at Greta.

"Right? Have you met him?"

"No. I haven't" she said.

The doorbell rang.

Kevin headed to the door.

"Well, you are about to."

We all congregated in the kitchen and around the bar, with Greta maintaining her sturdier seat. We shared wine and laughter from the start.

And Gabby seemed like such a different person around Calvin, she held on to him. She looked into his eyes when they talked, and her attention was never far away from him. And his actions mirrored hers. Ahhhhhh.

But of course, she saw my eye.

"What happened to you?"

Okay it was time to tell my girls that my ass was beat.

"Well, ladies, we must step away from mixed company first. Then and only then will I share the sordid details of my red eye!"

"Gents, get out!"

Gabby instantly sent them away. She looked at Calvin.

"We don't want Greta to have to get up." She said and kissed him. "Find another place, guys!"

They complied, turned on the TV and did some male bonding. I couldn't hear what they were saying. But I know they had interesting stories *if* they wanted to share.

"Okay," I said. "Let me tell you about my eye, my kidney, my body, my face. One word, Michelle!"

They both gasped.

"She was waiting for me the night we walked out together Gabby. We had a brutal fight."

"You are kidding!" Greta said shaking her head in disbelief.

"NO. When I got here, she was here, and one thing led to another. She beat my ass. But I beat her ass too," I said not to be outdone. "It was like fighting three young Mike Tysons, but me and pepper spray – thank God, made it even."

"I told you she was crazy, G" Gabby said.

Greta, shaking her head, seemed disappointed that we had fought at all.

"I know that," I said. I exhaled. "But I think it had to happen."

"What are you going to do now?" Greta asked.

"I filed a restraining order already. I don't know when she will be notified. But I think like all bullies, once a person stands up to them, they go away. She knows that she does not want any more of me."

"I thought you said *she* beat *your* ass!" Gabby exclaimed.

"She did! I also said I beat *her ass* too!"

"How did you beat her ass if she beat your ass?"

Greta laughed.

"Girl, I don't even want to tell you what she looked like when she walked away from me! People would think I won by a landslide!"

"It's not even about who won. Neither of you won! It's like you are trying to glorify fighting," Greta said. "I really hate this. Over a man!"

"See, that's where you are wrong, Greta. It was not over a man. I was fighting to protect myself. She's been bullying me for months. Do you think I wanted to fight? No! I did not!" I said, I was so pissed!

"But I chose not to run from her" I explained. "I chose to take the high ground and the high ground was to stand up for myself. Well, after she slapped me so hard that she literally knocked me off my feet. It was brutal."

Gabby shook her head.

"I knew it was coming. I just wish you had used the stun gun and got away from her." Gabby exclaimed. "Because it looks like she really did beat your ass! And is that a slap print on your face?!"

"I can't change it, Gabby. I wish I could, but I don't know what I would have done differently. Anyway, there you have it. Let's get the guys and have dinner. And yes! It is a slap print on my face! So what!?"

I walked away from them. I didn't want to talk about the fight ever again. So, we moved on…

It's amazing how six people with so much on their minds could sit together and have the most amazing dinner conversation. We laughed, we joked, we had so much common ground and we all really enjoyed the night. Exceptional.

Greta retired to bed almost immediately after a small desert and of course Cameron joined her. Gabby helped me tidy while Calvin and Kevin talked and watched the end of the football game. Pretty soon both Gabby and Calvin left.

(One Last Christmas Surprise)

Soon we were at the end of Christmas day and this superman of mine was resting in my bed and I was in his arms. He always felt like home. I could not ask for more. Sure, my ass had been beaten, but maybe that was the end to an era. I have more to be thankful for at this moment than I have in so many years. It's amazing that one person can change the entire trajectory of your life. This superman. He held me so closely. His kisses were from the clouds and heaven awaited us.

When his phone rang at this intimate moment, we were both a little surprised. After all it was after eleven o clock at night!

He reached to the bedside table took his phone, looked at it and an unusually concerned look appeared on his face.

"It's Doug. My ex-brother-in-law," he said.

He put the call on speaker.

"Hey, man. What's up?"

Doug answered quite stressed and just blurted out the facts, no buffer.

"Michelle overdosed, she's in the emergency room at General. I just wanted to tell you. She left you a note."

Dammit!!!

"How is she?" Kevin inquired, sitting up in bed.

"We don't know yet. But looks like she was in a fight too and she was beaten rather badly. She has scratch marks all over her face and arms. She has an injury to her hand; her eyes are red and swollen."

Kevin and I looked at each other – *Yikes!!! I guess I did beat her ass too!*

Doug continued, "She called a friend and told her that she had taken a handful of pills. Said she wanted to die. Her friend called 9-1-1 and she just got here. I was called and I called you."

"I'm not sure what you want me to do, Doug," he said and sat off the side of the bed.

"Well, I thought you would come out here, man! She tried to hurt herself because of you. She left you a note!"

Doug was beginning to sound angry.

"I know you think that whatever she did, she did because of me. But it was a decision *she* made. And I know you think rushing out there is what I should do. But I know it is not the best thing to do. And I know that I am not coming out there. However, if you don't mind, I would like for you to let me know how she is doing later. Keep me posted."

Doug abruptly discontinued the phone call.

Kevin looked at me.

I had nothing to say aloud. All I could think was WOW!

I just pray this was an attempt at manipulation.

I said a prayer for her.

I knew he did too...

To be continued...